Barry Crump wrote his fi[rst book, *A Good Keen]
Man,* in 1960. It became [a best-seller, as did]
numerous other books wh[ich followed. His most]
famous and best-loved New Zealand character is Sam
Cash, who features in *Hang on a Minute Mate*,
Crump's second book. Between them, these two
books have sold over 400,000 copies and continue to
sell at an amazing rate some 30 years later.

Crump began his working life as a professional
hunter, culling deer and pigs in some of the ruggedest
country in New Zealand. After the runaway success
of his first book, he pursued many diverse
activities, including goldmining, radio talkback,
white-baiting, television presenting, crocodile
shooting and acting.

As to classifying his occupation, Crump always
insisted that he was a Kiwi bushman.

He published 25 books and was awarded the MBE for
services to literature in 1994.

Books by Barry Crump

A Good Keen Man (1960)
Hang on a Minute Mate (1961)
One of Us (1962)
There and Back (1963)
Gulf (1964) – now titled *Crocodile Country*
Scrapwaggon (1965)
The Odd Spot of Bother (1967)
No Reference Intended (1968)
Warm Beer and Other Stories (1969)
A Good Keen Girl (1970)
Bastards I Have Met (1970)
Fred (1972)
Shorty (1980)
Puha Road (1982)
The Adventures of Sam Cash (1985)
Wild Pork and Watercress (1986)
Barry Crump's Bedtime Yarns (1988)
Bullock Creek (1989)
The Life and Times of a Good Keen Man (1992)
Gold and Greenstone (1993)
Arty and the Fox (1994)
Forty Yarns and a Song (1995)
Mrs Windyflax and the Pungapeople (1995)
Crumpy's Campfire Companion (1996)
As the Saying Goes (1996)
A Tribute to Crumpy: Barry Crump 1935–1996 is an anthology of tributes, extracts from Crump's books, letters and pictures from his private photo collection.

All titles currently (1997) in print.

A GOOD KEEN GIRL

Author's Note:
I've had a lot of trouble with the
carbon paper in the writing of this
book. It's been getting round the
wrong way all the time.

BARRY CRUMP

A GOOD KEEN GIRL

Illustrated by Tony Stones

Hodder Moa Beckett

". . . this godforsaken Blackrange, where the rocks float and the wood won't and the dogs do and the women don't . . ."

Bert Shambles, in the
Blackrange Station woolshed
during a flood.

First published in 1970 by A.H. & A.W. Reed

This edition published in 1997

ISBN 1-86958-545-3

© 1970 Barry Crump

Published by Hodder Moa Beckett Publishers Limited
[a member of the Hodder Headline Group]
4 Whetu Place, Mairangi Bay, Auckland, New Zealand

Typeset by TTS Jazz, Auckland

Cover photo: NZPL/J. Carnemolla

Printed by Wright and Carman (NZ) Ltd, New Zealand

Contents

ONE

THE BLACKRANGE STATION

In case anyone ever asks you where the Blackrange Station is, it's about sixty-five miles down the coast from the old whaling settlement of Pinderton, where the Blackrange River drops from 5,680 feet to the sea in less than eleven miles in a straight line. In the old days they'd clear-felled the bush, burnt it off, oversown the burns with grass, ringfenced the place, and built a big homestead, woolshed and implement shed from heart kauri brought down from the north.

They'd run as many as 10,000 merino-cross sheep and eleven hundred head of cattle on the nine thousand acres for the first few years, but by now all the place would support was one wild sheep to thirty acres, in the summer. In the winter some of them died off until it was supporting one sheep to forty-five acres. The cattle they'd left behind supported themselves by taking to the steep bush country towards the head of the valley and becoming very wild indeed.

There were a few goats and deer and wild pigs and possums on the property, but the climate kept their numbers to a minimum more effectively than the Noxious Animals Division could ever have done it.

In nineteen fifty-seven a pair of paradise ducks appeared on the big river flat about a mile and a half above the homestead, but there was a flood and they, too, had to abandon the place.

The East Coast Acclimatisation Society once stocked the

11

Blackrange River with 10,000 tagged rainbow trout fingerlings, but they might as well have fed them straight to the kahawai and kingfish at the rivermouth. When the Blackrange floods she really floods. The river can come up five feet in two hours and go down again just as quickly. Magnificent floods they are. Spectacular! Millions of tons of crumbling rock and shingle and dirt pours off the hillsides and cliff-faces every time it rains and the bar at the rivermouth gets wider and farther out into the sea every year. A trout wouldn't stand a chance.

A musterers' hut they'd once put in at the forks of the river, four hours' ride up from the homestead, was only ever used by the men who built it. When the musterers went up there the next season it was buried under thirty feet of shingle.

The Soil Conservation and Rivers Control Council had studied aerial photographs of the watershed and pronounced that the whole area was highly unstable and there was no known method of arresting the massive erosion, at this juncture. And the County Council Engineers had rejected the shingle from the Blackrange riverbed as unsuitable for roading purposes.

The Geology Department of the Victoria University has a map on which the Blackrange River Valley is marked as not suitable for mineralogical surveying, and the Commissioner of Crown Lands has reported that his department is unwilling to declare the area a national park on the grounds that the Associated Tramping and Mountaineering Clubs (Inc.) and the Search and Rescue Organisation, the Civil Defence people and the National Deerstalkers' Association have unanimously declared the area to be unsuitable for recreational purposes because of the dangers inherent in negotiating the higher slopes.

The Conservator of Forests' Field Research Crew once spent three days in the Pinderton pub and returned to the city to report that the Blackrange water catchment area was unsuitable for afforestation purposes in the foreseeable future, and the Noxious Weeds Inspector's report states that the whole valley is critically infested with ragwort, tutu, scotch thistle, bidi-bidi, barley grass, blackberry, gorse and manuka-blight.

The Lands and Survey Department, in nineteen sixty-one, submitted some soil samples from the Blackrange River Valley to the Department of Agriculture for analysing, and the Department of Agriculture advised the Lands and Survey Department that what topsoil was left was deficient in cobalt, copper, potash and phosphate, and required a minimum of fifteen hundredweight of lime to the acre in order to render it suitable for supporting even the hardiest of simple grasses. The Lands and Survey Department found that their resources were insufficient to bring the area into production.

The Rabbit Destruction Council, the Department of Scientific and Industrial Research, the Department of Maori Affairs, the Marine Department, the Mattress-makers' Union and the Wairapakau-North Ladies' Tatting Enthusiasts' Guild just weren't interested in the Blackrange Station. The best its seven hundred-odd Maori owners could do with it was lease it to me for two hundred dollars a year for twenty-one years, with a right-of-renewal for another twenty-one years, if I wanted it.

My name's Kersey Hooper and I knew what I was doing

when I took on the Blackrange Station. I'd had a good look over the place and, for a start, the homestead and buildings were in pretty sound condition. All they needed was cleaning up and a bit of repairing here and there. There was an old shearing plant in the woolshed that I was pretty sure I could get going again. And there were over two hundred sheep still running wild on the station itself and a couple of hundred head of wild cattle living along the bush ridges towards the head of the valley.

So I turned my mare out on the river flat, parked the Hudson under the macrocarpa behind the homestead, tied Sneak and the two pups under the woolshed, and shifted my gear into the homestead. Then I drove to the store eight and a half miles up the coast to arrange credit with the bloke who ran it.

As soon as he found out I'd taken over the Blackrange Station he knocked me back, but I had a bit of money to keep me going.

It took me nearly all the first week to get the stockyards and front paddock knocked into shape and glass put in some of the homestead windows. By this time I had myself fairly well organised. I was ready to start farming the place.

I ran the file over my knife and threaded the sheath on to my belt. Then I saddled the mare and put some things I'd got ready into the split-sack behind the saddle. Then I fed the pups and let Sneak off the chain and rode off up the valley.

The horse-track angled down to the riverbed and suddenly the distant sound of the surf on the coast was cut off, and there was only the vigorous grinding clinking and splashing rhythm of the horse's shoes on shingle as it carried me on up the valley, crossing and re-crossing the river from one flat to the next, and the occasional bleating of a sheep high up on the old burns above the river.

As I rode along I remembered odd snatches of conversation I'd had with some of the locals around the store:

"Where are you going to get your stock from?"

"There's a few wild cattle on the place. I'll use them to get me started."

"That's rich! There's wild cattle there all right. They're all through that bush along the Blackrange there. We get the odd one that comes out among our own cattle now and again, but we lose more than we ever gain."

"How come?"

"There's an old red bull. Been around here for years. Wanders through fences as though they're not there."

"He's taken a good few head of cattle back into the bush with him in the last few years."

"There's other bulls in there, some pretty big ones, too. But this old red joker seems to have the run of things. We've been trying to shoot him and run him down with the pig dogs, but he's always too cunning for us."

"You're welcome to any cattle you can get out of that bush, but you'll never keep any stock on the Blackrange Station as long as that old red bull's running around up there, I can promise you that . . ."

CHAPTER TWO
THE OLD RED BULL

The valley became closer and steeper. Thick bush took over from fern and scrub and the crossings were narrower and deeper. I had to swim beside the mare in several places and Sneak kept getting washed away.

Cattle sign. On a grassy flat at the forks of the main river and a fairly big side creek. Nothing fresh, not since the last rain anyway. I threw the saddle under a bank and hobbled the mare out on the flat. Then I threw a stone near Sneak for being interested in the scent of pigs and set off up the side creek.

About twenty minutes walking brought me to where a long steep spur came down from the main ridge at the head of the creek and I climbed up into heavy tawa bush. I cut myself a four-foot length of hard mature supplejack and gave Sneak a clout with it to try it out.

About five hundred feet higher up the ridge, where the tawa gave way to beech and ground-kiekie and crownfern, I took it easy. And then I saw a cattle beast. A cow, looking down at me from between her own astonished ears. She was lying down, on a rise about fifty feet ahead. I dug at Sneak with my stick and stood there without moving until the cow suddenly stood up and clambered off along a track that sidled away around the steep face.

I moved on and nearly at the top of the spur I smelt more cattle. They were lying around on a flat saddle in the ridge.

Three cows and two calves. Two of the cows were earmarked, but they didn't recognise me. When I quietly made them know I was there they plunged away over the edge of the ridge in a wild crashing panic.

It was just a little higher, where the spur ran out on to the main back ridge, that I found the old bull's sign. And along the ridge to the left the sign was no more than twenty-four hours old. And it was big sign. I poked around up there for the rest of the day but I couldn't find the old bull anywhere. When there was only an hour of sun left in the sky I sidled around on to a steep ridge and followed it down into a dirty creek-head. It was dark when I got back to the forks.

It was Sneak who found him. Middle of the next afternoon. Hiding in a patch of thick stuff, just over the edge of the main ridge. He was big all right. And he was red, with wide thick horns, and in no mood to be intruded upon. He stood motionless in his private tangle of vines and horopito.

I watched him for about a minute and then put Sneak on to him. The old bull snorted off along the ridge in the wrong direction, but Sneak pulled him up and turned him round before he got to the downhill slope on the other side of the watershed.

I dogged him hard every time he moved in the wrong direction and when he charged the dog we kept him going that way. And gradually I worked him over the edge of the ridge towards the heads of the side creek. Then a long sidle down across the steep creek-heads, dogging him hard whenever he got too far away or tried to climb. Down and across and back across the other way, right down into a branch of the side creek itself. And down the creek, dogging him hard every time he tried to climb out of it.

The old bull started getting frothy-mouthed, so I let him stand as long as I could afford. Then I eased him away towards the main river in the bottom of the valley, only dogging him when he went the wrong way or tried to think about turning back.

Where the creek began to open out towards the main river he suddenly charged the dog and then broke away up through the bush, climbing on an angle across a series of steep stony finger-ridges. I kept Sneak in. It was getting late.

I camped again at the forks.

Next morning the old bull was about a quarter of a mile along the main ridge from where we'd picked him up the day before. And he waited in some thick stuff until I was about thirty feet from him, and then he charged. Three-quarters of a ton of red bull suddenly came crashing and bellowing through the bush, tearing out vines and crushing everything in his way. I nipped quickly in behind a big red-beech and clouted him across the back with my supplejack as he floundered past me and wheeled away after Sneak, who'd dashed off to the other side of the ridge.

And so it started all over again. Down the side of the ridge, and sliding and crashing across the steep face of the watershed, easing the old bull down towards the creek. Wait — move him off — dog him away from the wrong direction — wait — dog him back out of there — losing height with every move.

And by early afternoon we had him back on the flat where

he'd broken away the night before, and he tried to do the same thing again. I had to dog him very hard to keep him there. This was where the old bull was going to make his stand.

I'd been keeping an eye on the sun and it was beginning to move off towards the western ridge, so I called Sneak off and stepped carefully out to let him have a go at me. And the old bull did. He'd been waiting for this all day. I got in behind a thick ribbonwood and clouted him with my supplejack as he ploughed past into a tangle of bush-lawyer and konini. He propped and slid round and charged again, snorting and rooting around my tree with a long rope of lawyer vine trailing from one of his horns. I kept the tree there and managed to slip the vine off his horn with the supplejack, cursing Sneak back out of it till he was told.

Round and back and past and through. A good clout across the nose or neck or back or rump with the supplejack every time he came boring in for another go. The bark on the ribbonwood hung in bruised strips from five feet to the ground. River stones were churned out of the ground to about fifteen yards out. I kept my eye on the sun and teased the old bull back again.

And after a while he got mad. He ran to a clump of waterfern at the bank of the creek and went down on his front knees and began bellowing and rooting into it with his horns. It's a pretty impressive sight when a big old bull like that goes frothy-mouthed on you.

My supplejack was shredded down to a shaving brush. I stepped out and waved and shouted to attract his attention, but he didn't hear me. So I ran up and slapped him on the rump with both hands, and he churned round and charged, twisting his head from side to side as he came, streaming saliva through the air, straight at me, tree and all. He hit the ribbonwood in full charge. I felt the shock of it jar my shoulder through the hand I had against my side of the tree. And then he moved away and stood there blowing dirt from his nostrils. He was getting tired.

I timed it right and got Sneak to come in wide and ease him in the direction of the main river. I brought the dog gently closer until the bull began to move, bellowing from side to side, down the creekbed. Then I left Sneak in charge and climbed a few feet up the side to cut myself a new supplejack.

And we eased that old bull right down the creek to the forks. At the junction he shambled out past the mare and waded into the river, where he stood, belly-deep and silent, watching me saddle up the horse.

I rode to the edge of the shadow on the river flat to see how much sun there was left. Then I waved Sneak out of the way and rode at the old bull from downstream. And when he came out to meet me I wheeled the horse in a light circle and sent Sneak in. We wheeled and zig-zagged and charged and propped. Down the flat and into the river and out on to the next flat and down to the next crossing, repeating the process almost move for move on each flat and crossing. I was getting the feel of this old red bull.

At a gorgy part of the river, where the valley was steep and narrow, I saw that we wouldn't get him much farther before dark. The whole of the valley floor was in shadow and the air was cold in my lungs. So as soon as he began to climb out on the far side of the crossing I called Sneak in behind and heeled the mare back on to the upstream bank.

I sat on a flat stone and looked across at the old bull, still standing where he'd stopped in the shallow water about seventy-five yards downstream, facing the other way. The mare cropped her way along the bush-edge, snorting into the grass every now and then. Sneak lay like a sphinx on the riverbank straight across from the old bull.

When it got dark I ate something out of the split sack and slept there on the stones, wrapped in the oilskin unbuckled from the knee-pad on the saddle.

In the morning the old bull was gone and I had to walk through the river to the next flat upstream to get the mare. Then I threw Sneak in behind with a stone and rode down river to find where he was hiding. It only took about an hour. Sneak knocked him up in a big grove of supplejack two hundred yards above the river on a finger-ridge three crossings downstream.

I dogged and supplejacked him down to the riverbed and eased him off down the valley. And when he had set his own shambling pace I moved in and increased it just enough so as to tire him but not enough to provoke him to turn and fight.

I ran him down the river and out into open country, and down to the wing that led into the stockyards, and into the stockyards, and straight through the rails at the far end of the stockyards, and through the fence on to the road, and up the middle of the road. And then a car came over the hill and my old bull blundered sideways through the road fence into some thick fern and over the bank, rolling and crashing and slithering down through thick secondgrowth on to the beach about thirty feet below.

I threw Sneak down after him to keep him busy until I got there and galloped round to the beach. And from then on it was simply a matter of running him back and forth along the beach until he'd quietened down enough to be supplejacked easy back up the road and over to the stockyards.

The old red bull had cut his load. He was footsore and tired, miles away from his home territory. He watched me fix the broken rails and didn't even charge when I walked right across the yard in front of him to put the staples and fencing pliers on the gatepost where I kept them.

It's a mystery to me how word about the bull got around but I was fixing the road fence next day when half a dozen of the locals pulled up in a truck to see for themselves. I headed them off before they got to the yards and spooked the old red bull. When I found out that they just wanted to have a look I let Sneak off the chain, just in case, and led them across to have their look.

"Hell's teeth! It's him all right!"

"Well look at that now. Talk about beginner's luck!"

"Yeah, we've been hunting this cunning old beggar for years, and you run into him first time you go out."

"And to top it off you bring him in alive!"

"I've never been lucky enough to run into him like that, but I wouldn't have bothered trying to bring him in. I'd have shot him where he was."

"But he's worth two hundred dollars, easy," I said.

"Where did you find him?"

"He was up on the back ridge."

"Fair go? How did you get him down here?"

"Just took my time."

"Did you have a rifle with you?"

"No, I use a lump of supplejack."

"What the hell would you do with a lump of supplejack if a bull this size charged you?"

"You just give him a clout with it," I explained.

"Ha ha ha!"

"Ha ha ha!"

"That's a beaut! Ha ha ha!"

"All jokes aside, how many dogs did you have with you?"

"Just this one," I said, kicking with my foot towards Sneak.

"Strike me pink, he must be a pretty good sort of a dog."

"What does he do?"

"He does what he's told," I said.

"Well now that we've rounded up this bloke the whole herd'll probably spread right out along the range."

But the next time I came down the river I brought four cows and two calves ahead of me.

In the first eight months I had the Blackrange Station I dogged and supplejacked and ran fifty-one very wild, very fit and very valuable head of cattle down to the yards. I had one or two close shaves with some of the cows, they're a bit tricky at times. But I sent four or five of them away at a time to the sales in Pinderton and made over three thousand three hundred dollars profit out of it. Eleven of the younger cows and a clean-looking bull I quietened down and kept in the homestead paddock to breed from.

I also mustered in two hundred and sixty-six ragged sheep and shore them in the woolshed. The ones I'd already done came in much easier the second and third times and brought more of the wild ones with them. By the end of the season I had three bales of wool ready to send away.

But it was hard going those first two seasons. There was so much to do. I shot all the wild rams I found and used them for dog-tucker, and bought a good Romney from the sale to breed from. I drenched the sheep and de-horned and inoculated the cattle. I bought an old tractor and fenced off two hundred acres of the best land, and put grass-seed and manure on it by hand. I planted fourteen hundred Lombardy poplar cuttings across the hillsides around the homestead. I bought hay to keep the stock going through the winter, and put six acres of river flat into rape and turnips. I painted the buildings and installed a diesel lighting plant and put in an electric stove to supplement the old wood-range in the homestead kitchen. And the bloke at the store eight and a half miles up the coast offered to open an account for the station.

I began to feel I'd made it. In the terms of stock, one animal to thirty acres, it wasn't enough to have impressed a bank manager, in fact it would have probably made him shudder, but when you consider the ratio of stock to the ratio of grass to the ratio of scrub and bare shingle and rock, it wasn't too bad. I was making a living out of it anyway.

I told you I knew what I was doing when I took on the Blackrange Station.

CHAPTER THREE

BERT

Half a mile down the road on the other side of the river Bert
and Betty Shambles milked a few cows and ran about fifty
head of dry stock and three hundred sheep on 400 acres of
what Bert described as rolling country along the coast. It
wasn't a hell of a good place as farms go, all Bert's paddocks
were about fifty acres and if he'd subdivided them into smaller
ones he'd have had to put in waterpipes and troughs.

He had a couple of weak bridges between the road and his
farm buildings and everything had to be hauled in and out in
small loads. There were open crossings he could use
sometimes, but whenever it rained they become raging
torrents, isolating the house and cutting off the only decent
lambing paddock on the place.

His fences were swept away in some places and hung
suspended above the ground in others. His top flats were
thickly covered with bidi bidi and ragwort. And down on the
flats around the self-drafting sheepyards and the woolshed,
which was well on the way to becoming a magnificent fernery,
he had a good coverage of barley grass and scotch thistles and
ragwort and mud.

There was one flat out the back that he could get about thirty
bales of hay and thistle to the acre off in a good season, but it
all had to be carted in, four bales at a time, on the packhorse,
and it was a tedious business.

No, the Shambles didn't have it easy by any means, but it never got them down. They weren't exactly what you'd call successful as far as farming went, but they weren't quitters and they didn't complain. They were my closest friends. I gave Bert help and advice about running and improving his farm, and Bert — well — Bert, in his own way, was just as much help to me.

Bert was no good out in the open where there was nothing to lean on. He had to have a tractor or a fence or a gate, or even something he could just put his foot up on, like the runningboard of the Hudson, while he talked endlessly about gigantic agricultural undertakings. And without his old felt hat on I think I'd have had to look twice to recognise him.

The only time Bert ever took his hat off was when Betty snatched it off his head when he was in the house, or when she caught him talking to women at the saleyards or somewhere. And Bert would be left groping awkwardly at where his hat had just been and whatever he'd been going to say would be lost forever. Betty told me she'd caught him sitting in the bath with his hat on once. And the only reason he hadn't been caught with it on in bed was because he wasn't game to forget to take his shirt off, and the hat came off when he pulled it over his head. He put them back on in the same order in the mornings.

Bert's wife Betty wasn't exactly the kind of woman you'd expect to get the pick of the bunch as far as men went, but she was a hell of a good worker and always bright and cheerful. She matched Bert's enthusiasm and optimism with big cheerful meals and batches of scones and things. Her kitchen in their ramshackle old house was a real good place to sit and talk, and Bert and I used to spend hours there while Betty pottered around getting us cups of tea and generally fussing about.

She'd have the shirt off your back and a new button sewn on or a torn pocket mended and the shirt tossed back to you by the time the kettle was boiling. And if you thanked her she'd just say "Pish!"

Betty loved animals. Every one of them. The sheep, the cows, the horses, the pigs — it just about broke her heart when some of the calves had to be sent away to the works every year, and the only thing she wouldn't do on the farm was bring in the killer hoggets for Bert and me to kill one for meat. Occasionally Bert would run across a condemned calf or dog-tucker ram hidden away in a gully up the back of the farm. An unofficial reprieve from Betty.

Wherever she went on their farm the animals would follow her. She always had an escort of calves, or pigs, or horses or cows, or a couple of hand-reared lambs whenever she crossed the paddock they were in. She had three goats tied to running wires along blackberry overgrown drains and fencelines and there was always a flurry of fowls and bantams around her back door. And at least half a dozen wild ducks flew in for a feed every time she went down to the duck-run to feed the ducks. Bert was always threatening to wait there with his shotgun one of these days, but he wasn't game to ever actually do it.

"The missus'd pack one on me if I did that, Kersey," he'd say, as though there was no more terrifying prospect.

33

I'd never seen Betty "pack one" and when I asked Bert if she ever had, it didn't look as though he'd ever seen it either. But it was good for him to have something to be scared of.

Betty always gave any sick animals priority, even over Bert. She'd often fuss till midnight, with lambs in boxes and on sacks all over her kitchen, during the lambing. And she'd sit up with a calving cow in trouble until everything was all right, no matter how long it took.

Bert once confided to me that he was scared to let on when he was sick or hurt because of the tremendous fuss Betty always made of him. But I noticed once that when Bert was trying to dodge the milking with a phoney dose of double-pneumonia Betty had him out of the house and down to the cowshed before he'd even finished telling her about his symptoms.

I'll never forget when we got the telephone put through our district. Five of us had agreed to clear the line across our properties for them and I got the thick end of the stick. They surveyed it right across two really dirty gullies, full of thick scrub and fern and second growth and steep as hell. And then it went up through another lot of thick stuff across the river and down to the road on the other side of the ridge to opposite Bert's place. Then it crossed the road and travelled across Bert's paddocks to Bert's house.

And there it stopped because between Bert's house and his neighbour's boundary was a great hillside of tangled gorse and blackberry and fern and manuka that Bert hadn't cleared the line through yet.

This served to make Bert the most popular man in the whole district, compared with his popularity two months later, when he still hadn't cleared the line through his property. By this time the Post and Telegraph gang had packed it in and gone back to Pinderton and nobody seemed to know whether or when they were coming back.

By this time both Bert and I had the telephone on, but four places further down the line were still waiting for theirs because Bert hadn't cleared his line. In fairness to Bert it must be said that he wasn't ignoring the problem. He made starts on cutting a line through that scrub in four different places, to my knowledge. But for one reason or another he never got very far.

Then one day Bert's neighbour, a bloke called Mick Spinell, came slashing his way out of the scrub behind Bert's house. He'd cut the line himself. Bert was over at my place at the time but, according to Betty, Mick wouldn't even stay for a cup of tea. He must have wanted that telephone pretty badly. Bert had told Mick he could use his phone any time he wanted it, but Mick had never taken advantage of the offer.

"He must want a telephone of his own," said Bert. "Possessive beggar."

It was another four months before the telephone line was completed and all eight of us had the telephone on. It's hard to be angry with Bert for very long. He's so disarming, but for a long time I was the only one who would speak to Bert on the telephone.

Bert's phone was never a great success for him anyway. He

never really got the hang of using it properly. He shouted as though there was no telephone there at all, and he always blamed the woman on the exchange when he couldn't ring the right number.

It was Betty who finally told me the terrible truth about Bert and telephones. He was nervous of them. Every time his phone rang he leapt violently, as though he'd been waiting for it, and then he'd dash to answer it, no matter whose ring it was. For the first few weeks whenever anyone rang the exchange or the code of another number on the line Bert would snatch the hand-piece off the phone and demand to know what they wanted. And he was so nervous and suspicious about the whole process that it was often very difficult to get him off the line. He'd want to know who you were ringing up and what you were ringing them up for. Then he'd demand to know why the hell you didn't go and see them yourself, if you wanted to talk to them.

"I don't know, Kersey," he said, bending to uproot a ragwort plant at his feet and hang it on the fence in front of him. "If I've got something to say to a man I like to say it to him personally. These bloody telephones, now. They only give a man the chance to back out of it as though he'd never said it in the first place."

I tried to explain that the telephone was a very useful instrument and could save him a lot of money, but Bert couldn't see it. As a matter of fact I got the impression that he was quite relieved when they came out one day and disconnected his phone. After all, all he had to do to get it put on again was apologise to the woman on the exchange for some suggestion he'd made to her involving an enema. But he never bothered. Bert's telephone career lasted just ten months and its termination was a great relief to everyone on the line, including Bert himself.

"If that noxious-weed bloke ever comes near my place again I'll shoot the bastard in his tracks," Bert said to me one day, shoving a notice at me that said he had twenty-one days to clear the ragwort off his property.

But this wasn't really as menacing as it may sound. The Noxious Weeds Inspector was as safe as Bert's ragwort, and if you could have seen Bert's ragwort and balanced it against the resources he had to clear it off his property, you'd know that the Noxious Weeds Inspector had nothing to worry about.

If I'm ever going to have to be shot, either by design or accident, I want Bert to do it, because regardless of the circumstances or the conditions; regardless of the range; regardless of the thousands of rounds of various calibred ammunition he's detonated over the years; regardless of the science and technology that's gone into the design and manufacture of the modern firearm and the variable-powered, gas-filled telescopic sight; regardless of the great strides that have been made in the field of ballistics since he first started shooting; regardless of the three years he spent in the army; regardless of the fact that he rides off up my valley almost every Sunday to drop the odd pig or two, just to keep his eye in; regardless of the eleven-point trophy head hanging on his cowshed, that he shot at a fantastic nine hundred yards in a blizzard; regardless of the fact that he handles a rifle or shotgun with the practised flourish that only comes to a man after a lifetime of continuous experience, Bert would miss me.

He's the most terrible, barrel-stretching, range misjudging, rifle-blaming, wounded-him-but-he-just-got-away-saying, ammunition-wasting, plain lousy shot I've ever known in my life. He couldn't hit a cow in the backside with a wet spade — or a bull in the bum with a handful of rice, for that matter. But as soon as anything shootable appeared Bert would instantly begin shooting at it, and he'd keep on shooting at it until one of two things happened: either he'd run out of ammunition, or the target would move out of sight, whichever occurred first.

I never knew him to hit anything. I've known him empty a twelve-shot magazine at a possum sitting on his gatepost and then run back to the house for more ammunition. The first time we ever went out hunting together he clean missed a standing goat at twenty yards, and then, a bit later, his confidence completely unscathed, he slung up his rifle and fired at a stag we'd spotted standing on the ridge nearly three quarters of a mile away.

"How's that!" he said, excitedly working the bolt of his rifle.

The stag didn't move.

"I think you might have missed him that time," I said.

"Hang on!" And he fired again,

"How's that then!" he said triumphantly.

The stag lowered his head and went on feeding.

"I don't think he's seen us yet, Bert," I said. "Let's ride a bit closer. We might be able to sneak up on him."

"Remind me to shoot this bloody rifle of mine in, Kersey. I think she's shooting a bit low and to the left."

He used eighty shotgun cartridges on the opening day of the

duck-shooting season one year, and was back home in time to help Betty finish the milking without having ruffled a feather. There were nine shooters around the swamp that morning and they bagged one duck and one pukeko all told. Apparently over a hundred and fifty ducks flew in but none of them landed. Bert would start blazing away as soon as they appeared over the horizon and he'd frightened them all away. He apparently frightened the other shooters too. The ranger offered to refund Bert's shooting-licence fee on condition he kept away from the swamp on opening day of the duck season in future, but Bert wasn't going to be put off like that. He had as much right to his bit of sport as anyone else, and he thoroughly enjoyed it, too.

"A man's got to have a go, Kersey," he'd say, dry-shooting a rocketing blackbird with his slasher with such an easy-flowing flourish, complete with recoil, that I'd half-expect to hear the blast of the shot and see the blackbird suddenly disintegrate in a shower of feathers.

It was the same when Betty and Bert and I went kahawai fishing at the mouth of the Blackrange River. Bert would stride forward with his line coiled expertly in one hand and the spoon swinging easily from the other. Then he'd stand there inscrutably surveying the rip at the rivermouth for a while. Then he'd glance at the sky, move a few feet to one side or the other, and begin to swing the spoon in a steadily increasing circle around himself. Then he'd let her go, and his line would fairly sizzle out across the water, to land anywhere from fifteen to a hundred and fifty feet out. Then he'd begin to retrieve it with a long expert rhythm that brought six feet of line in with every sweep of his arm.

But as soon as he got a strike all his poise and concentration and co-ordination and experience and skill left him with a sudden shout.

"Kersey! I've got one! Quick! It's a whopper! A monster! Kersey! It must be a kingi! It'll smash my gear up! I can't hold him! Quick! Kersey! No, it's all right! Here he comes! I've got him! No! He's too big! Come here you bastard — sorry Betty — I've got him I think! This is a big one, Kersey!"

And he'd churn back and forth on the stones and end up to his knees in the water and have to scramble back from a wave with all his slack line trailing in a tangle from one of his boots. And if by this time the fish hadn't got off, he'd pull a big silver kahawai curving and flopping up out of the surf and on to the stones, where he'd kick and shovel it up the beach to the flat level above high water. And then, breathlessly triumphant, he'd pounce on it and subdue it. Then he'd hold it up for us to see.

"How's that, Kersey? What do you reckon this one'd go? Twelve pounds?"

"Pretty close to it, Bert," I'd say.

And then Bert would start to untangle his line, but as soon as Betty or I hooked another fish he'd drop his line and run through it to help.

"Hold him, Betty! Don't let him have any slack line! You'll lose him! What are you doing, woman? There, you've gone and lost him! No you haven't. You've got him! Now bring him in! Not too fast or you'll tear the hook out of his mouth! That's it! Don't muck around with him, bring him in! There! You've got him!"

And Bert would stand over the vanquished fish as though he'd done it all by himself singlehanded.

"How many's that we've got, Kersey?" he'd say.

"Four, counting your one."

"Good, we'll smoke this lot if we get enough of them."

And he'd return to untangling his line until the next strike was announced. Often, by the time Bert had his line untangled, Betty and I would have landed four or five kahawai each, but that didn't worry Bert. He got a great kick out of fishing, no matter who caught them.

It was the same with hunting. Whenever I got something, whether it was a deer or a pig or even only a goat for the dogs, Bert would be genuinely pleased and excited about it. Just as he was proud of the way I was making a living off the Blackrange Station, when everyone else had said I wouldn't last six months. He used to tell everybody about how many cattle I'd brought in out of the bush and the things I'd done as though he'd played a major part in it himself.

And he had. There's nobody more enjoyable to be in the company of than someone who's enjoying themselves.

CHAPTER FOUR
HEREPO

The first I knew about Herepo was when this Maori joker drove up on the old Ferguson tractor he used for a car. I found out later that he'd got the tractor in return for some fencing he was doing for a cow-cocky along the coast in his spare time. The brakes on this machine were so shot that all his weight on the pedals was insufficient to put them on hard enough to stop him on the flat. I wondered at the time how he got on when he had to stop going downhill, but he explained later that he never started going downhill unless he intended going *all* the way down.

He was wearing a pair of blue overalls under a yellow plastic raincoat and a red bushman's safety-helmet with an American eagle scratched through the paint to the aluminium on the front of it. He wore two dog collars buckled in sequence for a belt, and a leaky-looking pair of gumboots. He was about forty-five to sixty-five years old, I suppose. It was pretty hard to tell.

He slowly descended from his seat on the tractor and extended a hand covered with faded tattoos that had obviously been done with a needle and some marking ink.

"G'day," I said, shaking hands with him.

"Kia ora, boss," he said.

"What can I do for you?" I said.

"I come to get my old job back again, boss."

"What job's that?"

"On the station, boss. The Blackrange."

"Don't tell me you used to work here."

"Too right, boss. I worked here when they close her up."

This was interesting. "How long ago was that?" I asked him.

"Long time ago now, boss. I was just a young feller."

"Who was running the place then?"

"The boss, boss."

"Yeah, well what made them close the place down?"

"Floods, boss. Water everywhere. She wash all the sheep away. No sheep, no shear, no money, no job. But the boss she told me when the Blackrange get on her feet we all get our job back. So when I hear she started up again I come for my job."

"Do you mean to say a woman ran this place?" I said.

"No, boss. The boss was the boss. Her missus look after the house. The boss run the station."

"How long ago was that?"

"About thirty year, boss."

"How long were you working here?"

"Five weeks, boss."

"You worked here for five weeks thirty years ago, and now you've come to get your job back?"

"Yes, boss. The boss told us we get our job back when the Blackrange start up again."

"Well what can you do?"

"Anything, boss"

"Okay, I'll give you a week's trial. You can sleep in the back bedroom in the house. That suit you?"

"I don't know if I can stay for a whole week, boss. My brother-in-law needs me for the kumaras. I come back after."

46

And that was how I met Herepo. He worked for me for four days but you couldn't see where he'd been. Not that he was a straight-out loafer, he always *seemed* to be working but it was really that he worked very hard wasting time. He never actually got anything done. It's hard to explain. I paid him and he drove off on his Ferguson to see his brother-in-law about the kumaras.

The next thing I heard about Herepo was that he'd swiped a truck with a whole family on the back from outside the Pinderton pub and driven it to Seaforth to pick up a second-hand coil for his old tractor. He got back and walked into the pub and the bloke who owned the truck and the family didn't know they'd been all the way to Seaforth and back during the past three hours. He only found out about it when his truck ran out of gas on his way home that night.

I didn't really expect to see Herepo again after that but blow me down if he didn't turn up again about a month later, asking for his old job back again. He'd been working for a logging contractor and had been very unfairly treated. Herepo was most indignant about it.

"She's a crook boss, that one, boss," he said. "Last time I work for that one."

"What'd he sack you for, anyway?" I asked him.

"The tractor I drive for him," said Herepo. "She bloody hard to start when you let her get cold, eh. So I save some time for the boss, on Saturday I fill her up with diesel and leave her idling. On Monday morning she still idling, all warmed up and ready to start work. But the boss she says I waste his money. It's down the bloody road for me."

47

"It's a bit tough, all right, Herepo," I said.

"If that boss ever comes to me and says, 'Herepo, I need you to drive my bulldozer,' I say to him, 'No, boss, you drive the bloody thing yourself.' She's a crook boss, that one, boss," concluded Herepo.

Herepo stayed nearly three weeks that time. He was too scared of cattle to be much help with them. In fact he was even a bit chary of the sheep, or maybe it was just the work that was involved. He *could* work though. In fact he wasn't too bad at fencing, but I had to be there all the time to keep an eye on him and keep him moving. So all I got out of employing Herepo was a break from actually having to do all the work myself, which was worth it in a way, even though I could have done it quicker and better myself.

Herepo was as superstitious as hell. He had to have a candle burning beside his bed all night, in case of Kehuas. And everything had an old Maori legend attached to it. Like, a sun-shower meant that an old person had died and the world was weeping with sadness at the loss, and the sun was shining because it was pleased to welcome another soul into the Spirit World. And if Herepo had had his way everything would have been painted red, because red keeps the Patupaiarehe away.

He'd save hours of work from getting done by telling you Maori legends about things, and whether he was making them up as he went along I don't know, but he never ran out of them.

A fantail would arrive on the job and start flitting around. Herepo would stop working and say,

"Ha, Tiwakawaka!"

"Ti-what?" I'd say.

And before we could get on with the job I'd have to be told how the fantail used to be a very sluggish little fellow in the old days. And one day a Maori joker who was looking all over the place for where fire was hidden got the wheeze that the fantail knew. So he grabbed the fantail and squeezed its head between his finger and thumb to make it talk. The fantail hung on as long as it could, until its eyes were nearly popping out and its tail spread and stuck out from its body. Then it spilt the beans and told the Maori that fire was hidden in the kaikomako tree. All he had to do was get a couple of hunks of kaikomako wood and rub them together and he'd get fire.

So the Maori joker got his fire and the fantail got sticking-out eyes and a spread-out tail, but the fantail doesn't mind because he can see everywhere at once and flit around in the air getting big feeds of insects.

By the time Herepo had told me all this it'd be time to swing the billy for lunch, and Herepo would prolong the lunch break with a yarn about how the mosquito and the sandfly first decided to attack man. It seems the sandfly got a bit impatient on it and got stuck in during the day, and suffered heavy losses. But the old mossie was more cunning and waited until it got dark. That way he avenges at night the damage done during the day to his friend the sandfly.

I got to like old Herepo and his stories but he was something of a luxury to employ because I never got any extra work done while he was working for me and I still had to pay him and feed him. He never stayed long, though, and I was always glad to see him when he came jouncing along on his old Ferguson to get his old job back again.

Herepo wasn't all fairytale and fable, either. He had a lot of sound, practical knowledge under his safety-helmet. He didn't trot it out very often, though, because there was a very definite risk of it involving him in work.

For example there was the young rimu tree I'd carefully wrenched and then transplanted from a patch of native bush up the valley to the front yard of the homestead. It wasn't picking up very well at all and I had an idea it was very nearly dead.

"Don't know what I'm going to do about that young rimu," I said to Herepo one day. "It looks more like a firewood job every day. I must have broke too many roots when I transplanted it."

"No, boss," he said. "It's not the roots."

"What is it then?"

"It's lonely, boss."

"*Lonely?* How do you mean?"

"It's on its own, boss. Put another rimu there and they both grow together."

So when we were coming back down the valley on the tractor we brought another young rimu and planted it beside the first one.

"Do you really think there's anything in this business of trees getting lonely, Herepo?"

"Too right, boss. You never see the Maori plant one tree on her own, eh?"

I had to admit I hadn't. And within a few weeks both rimus were coming away nicely.

Herepo occasionally did a bit of work for Bert. They enjoyed working together but it was bad for any job they took on. It took the pair of them two full days to put a new stay on the strainer post at Bert's road gateway. They spent most of the time Maori-legending or giving great long-winded sets of confused directions to passing motorists. Or fishing down at the rivermouth.

We were all down there fishing one day and Bert said, "Tide's coming in fast."

And Herepo said, "Yes, Tangaroa breathes out this morning."

"Who does what?" said Bert.

"Tangaroa, the sea god," said Herepo. "He lies very still in the deepest part of the sea, sleeping. The Maori says that when Tangaroa breathes in, all the water gets drawn into his body and the tide is low. When he breathes out the water is all pushed out again and makes the full tide. Every now and then Tangaroa gives the big sigh, that is how spring tides are made."

"Do you really believe all that stuff about gods and legends and things?" asked Bert.

"My ancestors were too busy to think about things that couldn't be explained," said Herepo. "So he made it easy for his children to understand by passing on these legends. Then he could get on with his work."

Coming from Herepo, this statement was a bit ripe, but actually Herepo agreed with work, in principle.

One day he said to me, "Bert is like the kikihi, eh boss?"

"What's that?" I said, abandoning the idea of getting started for a while yet.

"The cicada, boss, the kikihi. You are the little ant, the popokorua."

"How do you make that out, Herepo?"

"In the summer there's plenty of kai, eh," said Herepo. "And the old kikihi he sits on the bark singing all the time. But the little popokorua he working, working all the time. Never stop. And when the winter comes the kikihi gets cold. All the leaves fall off the trees. The kikihi dies, boss. But the little popokorua he stays fat and warm in his whare and waits till the summer comes again."

"What's that got to do with Bert and me?" I said.

"When the big floods come you will be able to keep your animals alive because you have worked hard in the summer, boss. But Bert he will lose his sheep and cows because he spends his summer singing on the bark."

"Well what about you," I said. "Where do you fit into it?"

"I'm the koekoea, boss. The long-tailed cuckoo. I can migrate, eh. I go where it's warmer and there's no floods."

And he did, too. He went winging off on his tractor just before the first floods of winter and we didn't see him again until most of the damage had been cleared up the following spring.

CHAPTER FIVE
A Spell Away

Now it wasn't that I was distrustful in those days, or afraid of getting involved or committed, or anything like that. And it wasn't a matter of not being able to afford it. It wasn't that it clashed with any strong religious beliefs I held, either, because I didn't hold any strong religious beliefs. Nor was there anything to indicate that I'd been badly treated by a wicked stepmother or older brothers or sisters or sadistic aunts when I was a young feller. Nobody's suggesting anything like that for a moment. It was more likely that I just hadn't had the time. But the fact remains that at the age of thirty-three I'd never really had much to do with women.

Bert tried to pair me off with a woman he wintered a couple of riding hacks for one winter. He even used to chase her horses into my place so the woman and I would get acquainted. I gave her a hand to catch a bay gelding once, and tacked a set of shoes on it for her over at Bert's place, but nothing happened.

No, I might have had the edge on Bert as far as farming was concerned, but when it came to women Bert could run rings round me.

It seems that when Bert was a young bloke he had some kind of fatal attraction that made him irresistible to women. Cursed with an indefinable something that caused them to pursue him with all the relentless scheming purposefulness of

55

their sex, Bert had apparently only managed to keep his relationships with them on a perpendicular basis by sheer decency and willpower.

He'd had to flee from fifteen-year-old viragos! He'd been hounded by wanton harridans of eighteen and nineteen. They converged on him. They followed him. They waylaid him in dark lanes and hallways. They stalked him at work. They fought over him at parties. They queued up for him. They shared him at picnics. They set traps for him. They tried to seduce him in cars and picture theatres. They wore "negligences" for him. They engulfed him at seasides. They forced money and gifts on him. They invited him on world cruises in private motor yachts. They offered him managing directorships of huge business corporations . . .

But by sheer good fortune and his own nimblewittedness he'd managed to hang on, right up to the age of nineteen, when Betty had arrived on the scene and finally brought him to bail up against the wall in the cloakroom of a country dance hall.

Of course he fought against it. He dodged and avoided her. He tried to make her ashamed of him. He even lost her in a bet with one of his mates, but eventually he'd had to give up the unequal struggle, and just seven months after she'd first ambushed him, Betty led Bert off to the altar. And they'd been living and working together ever since, quite contentedly, as far as I could see.

"No, Kersey," said Bert, carefully picking an invisible piece of fluff from the lapel of his bush singlet and flicking it out of the woolshed, "Women have been my downfall, there's no doubt about that. I still have to be careful with 'em sometimes."

"Careful?" I said.

"Yeah. Mind you I'm not saying they're all bad," he hastened to reassure me. "Get a good one and you're set for life. Take yourself, for example."

"Me?"

"Yeah. What you need is a good wife, Kersey. Someone to help you on the station. To do the cooking and washing and look after you. Make a home for you. Someone to share the future with, and breed from. A good keen girl, that's what you need."

"A good keen girl?"

"Yep, a good keen girl. There's nothing to beat 'em, if you can get a good one."

I'd been doing a fair bit of work on the station the year I want to tell you about. Mostly giant-discing and ringfencing forty acres of rough stuff up the valley to run a few head of dry stock on next season. That's not counting all the other work that had to be kept up around the place. And I decided to take a holiday.

I had the back seat out of the Hudson for carting bales of hay and the odd sheep and stuff like that, so all I had to do was throw a few extra spares and tools and gear into her and take off. Bert was keeping an eye on the station and feeding the fowls and dogs for me. I did the same for them when they went away.

I didn't have any idea where I was heading for, it didn't matter all that much. I just felt like having a spell away from

57

the station. It was the first time in over four years I'd been away for any length of time. I turned north on the main highway, twelve miles past Pinderton, because it was a fair while since I'd been up that way. But I'd only gone forty miles past the turnoff when I started having a bit of trouble with the car. I had her running a bit lean because they're inclined to hog the gas, those old jobs. It was okay for the bit of running around I'd been doing, back and forth between the station and the store, but the long run had overheated her and she was starting to stink and fume.

I pulled up and opened the mixture screw on the main jet half a turn. There was a bit of steam hissing out of the radiator overflow and the block was crackling with the heat, so I waited there for a while to let her cool down a bit. But not long after I got going again she started missing a bit and great clouds of white steam began pouring out all over the place. What water there was left in her was being shoved out through the exhaust. I'd done the head gasket in for certain, and I wasn't going to get much further before she seized up on me all together.

There was a scattering of shops and light industrial buildings along the road just there and when I saw a motel I swung in and turned her off. And before I'd even stopped the car a bloke who couldn't tell the difference between smoke and steam came belting out of a doorway, shouting and waving for me to get it away from the buildings.

He settled down when I explained and I asked him if I could park up somewhere and repair the damage. The motel bloke said they weren't officially open for business yet but he thought they'd be able to accommodate me, seeing as I was in a spot. We pushed the Hudson in between a couple of motel units in a long row of them.

Then the motel bloke opened the door of a unit with a key and said, "You can use this one. Drop over to the office and pay your deposit when you're settled in."

I hadn't actually thought about booking into the place but it wasn't such a bad idea, come to think of it. It was a pretty simple sort of a set-up. Two rows of units, built along the lines of a cowshed. Concrete blocks with corrugated aluminium roofing, alloy window frames and concrete flagstones. Low stud, and the walls facing the road had been plastered with the mixture a bit on the dry side. The soil was mostly clay and a bit sour-looking. Probably needed lime. They'd planted some small trees and shrubs around but they weren't coming away very well. Might pick up next season with the right manure.

Inside, the unit was about the size of a decent pump shed. They'd lined it with softboard and the floor was lino-tile over poured concrete with a few mats scattered around. They'd butted a couple of hardboard partitions against one end wall to make three alcoves. There was a shower rigged up in the middle one and a lavatory at the far end. They had a small low-voltage stove rigged up in the other cubicle, with a sink, a bench and cupboards and cooking gear. There were two single beds in the main part of the unit and that's about all there was to it. If anyone had used the place before me they hadn't left any sign of it. It was a good a place as any to do the Hudson up.

I took some of my stuff into the unit and went over to pay the motel bloke his deposit and ask if I could use their telephone. It was a more complicated way of ringing up than the party line I was on at the station and I had to try several wreckers in Seaforth, a fairly big town twenty-six miles away. Eventually I got onto a bloke who reckoned he had what I wanted, a '37 Chrysler one. I had an idea they were interchangeable so I got him to send it out with a carrier who did a daily run past the motel, just in case I couldn't get what I wanted in the meantime. I couldn't.

It took me most of the afternoon to get the head off the Hudson. It didn't look as though she'd had a spanner near her since she left the factory. Makes a man wonder how they keep going sometimes. The valves looked all right, as far as looks go. It doesn't pay to poke around with them when they're like that, you never know what might happen.

I sat the head back on the studs and left everything alone till the new gasket arrived. The old one was certainly blown, but as far as I could tell that was all that was wrong with her.

The motel bloke came over to invite me to join him and his family for a meal at around six o'clock. I hadn't thought about eating until just before that. I thanked him and we stood around talking until his old lady called out that it was time for him to start getting the dinner on. I had a clean up and put on the blue shirt Bert and Betty had given me for some Christmas or other.

On the way over to the motel bloke's house, at one end of a row of his motel units, I stopped for a look at a couple of fairly big pines that were leaning all over the place just inside the back fence. They'd cut out a whole windrow of them by the look of it, and left just these two trees standing. Nasty-looking things they were, liable to fall anywhere. It didn't make sense.

The motel bloke took me into their sittingroom and gave me a knockdown to his old lady. He was a skinny little bloke but she was carrying a fair bit of condition. Then the motel bloke broke out a bottle of beer and we sat round yarning for a while. From what the old lady said I gathered that they had a daughter running around somewhere who was due to turn up at any time. She came in a bit later and helped herself to a glass of beer. The way they'd been talking about her I'd been expecting a schoolgirl, but she was a full-grown woman. We shook hands and she parked her frame on the other end of the sofa I was sitting on.

She wasn't a bad looker, in a pale sort of a way. Big round eyes the colour of a treated pine post and skin like a bucket of beastings. Didn't look as if she got much sun. Her hair was the same gingery colour as a new boot and she was fairly tall with long feet and hands but a bit herring-gutted on it. She never had much to say for herself.

Their name was Chadwick. The old man was Alby, the old lady was Mrs Chadwick and the daughter's name was Faith.

Alby opened another bottle of beer and then went into the kitchen to see how the tucker was getting on.

The old lady was a tiger to talk. She told me all about how they'd had a little business of their own in Seaforth and sold it to build the motel. They'd only been in the place for a few weeks and hadn't got it properly under way yet. She'd been married once before and had to divorce her first husband for deserting her. Left here alone and defenceless until Alby had turned up. The daughter had arrived about a year after they were married and the three of them had been a team ever since.

But it didn't look to me as though there was much teamwork going on. Alby was hogging all the work.

"Now, tell us something about yourself, Mr Hooper," said the old lady, grabbing at my arm. "What line of business are you in?"

I told them a bit about how I'd taken over the Blackrange Station and then Alby came in to say the tucker was on the table and we went into the kitchen and got stuck into it. It was a pretty good feed, too. He'd roasted up a leg of mutton and slung a few spuds in with it. There was quite a bit of other stuff going but I settled for another lash at the mutton and spuds.

"I suppose you must get quite a lot of meat on your farm," said the daughter.

"Too right," I told her. "My mate Bert and I have got on to a great lurk with the killer mutton. Guarantee the meat'll be as tender as you can get it every time."

"Really?" said the old lady. "You'll have to let us in on your little secret, Mr Hooper. Some of the meat we get from our butcher is as tough as old boots."

"Well, when you're going to kill a sheep for mutton," I explained, "you always want to shut it up in the yard with a few of its mates for a day or two, to let it settle down and get used to being handled, lets 'em empty out a bit too. If you run a sheep in off the hill and grab it and cut its throat while it's all nervous and worked up it's ten to one the meat'll be tough. And it's harder to make a clean job of it when they're kicking around, too."

The old lady thanked me for the tip and reckoned she was going to pass it on to her butcher next time she saw him.

CHAPTER SIX
BENDY AND UGLY

After Alby had cleaned up his kitchen we sat around yarning in the lounge. The old lady and the daughter went to bed around eight o'clock and Alby and I opened another bottle of beer and got to talking about the motel and the problems connected with getting it under way.

"You want to knock those two pines out there down for a starter," I told him. "If they come this way in a storm or something they'll flatten some of your buildings."

It turned out that Alby had got a pretty rotten deal from the contractors who were supposed to have cleaned up the row of pines for him. They'd felled the rest of them and then held out for another hundred dollars when they saw how tricky the last couple were going to be.

"They'd have gone over easy enough if they'd nicked 'em and dragged 'em in the right direction with some of the easier trees," I told him. "They've made work for themselves. Don't pay them till they've finished the job."

But it wasn't as simple as that. They'd slapped up a couple of shops on the only section where trucks or tractors or a crane could get access to the trees. The contractors weren't even asking him to pay them for the work they'd done, but they wouldn't touch those two trees at any price. And now the council was putting the pressure on Alby to remove them because of them being dangerous. There were a couple of houses behind the motel that might cop it if they fell away from the motel itself and according to Alby the owners weren't all that terribly happy about it.

In the end I told Alby I'd have a look at his trees in the morning and see if anything could be done with them.

It was still pretty early when I got back to my motel unit so as long as I was waiting around I decided I might as well bring the head of the Hudson inside and scrape a bit of the carbon off it. I found a file and a wire brush in the waggon and got stuck into it. It was a bit tough on the motel sink bench but I could clean that up later. What had me a bit worried was that she was more carboned-up than I'd thought and when I had it scraped clean I found a couple of high spots. In fact it looked as though the head itself was slightly warped.

So I started to carefully draw-file the whole blasted head, but it was a very delicate operation, under the circumstances, and they only had a forty-watt bulb in the motel unit. I needed more light on the job. One wrong drag, a bit too heavy in the wrong place and I'd score the head and ruin it completely.

The Chadwicks' Austin was parked just outside the window so I got some wire out of the Hudson and unscrewed one of their sealed-beam headlights and rigged up a lead-light from their battery, passed it in through the window and propped it up on the bench beside me. It worked perfectly but it was a quarter past two in the morning by the time I got it finished, and I still had a hell of a mess to clean up.

It was no use putting the headlight back in the Chadwick's Austin without lining it up properly for them, so I pulled the wires off the battery and put the whole caboodle under the bed where it wouldn't get broken. Then I had to siphon a bit of gas out of the Hudson to clean up the bench with, but when I got the grease and oil and carbon cleaned off I found that the bench surface hadn't stood up to the work as well as I'd thought it would. In fact it was pretty badly scored where I'd been shifting the head round on it.

In the end I decided it wasn't worth upsetting the Chadwicks at this stage, so I unscrewed the whole bench, sink and S-bend and all, and replaced it with a brand new one, from the unit at the far end of the row, for them.

By the time I'd got the window screwed back on the end unit it was getting daylight, so I decided to go out and have a look at old Alby's trees while no one was around. It was still pretty dark but you could see the trees easy enough. Radiata pine, about thirty years old, by the look of them. They'd grown long and spindly, sheltered by the ones that had grown up around them. No big branches on the trunks of them but they were both top-heavy as hell. Looked like two nasty bends in the barrel of one tree and the other had a slight lean towards the corner of Alby's house and a heavy belly dragging it out towards one of the houses across a right-of-way behind the motel. They were going to be tricky all right. There was nowhere to even get a tie-back.

On its own each tree was just too dicey to be worth the risk, but if I nicked the ugly one and left plenty of wood at the motel side of the scarf to drag her back as she went, and then cut the bendy one nearly through and wedged it over into the ugly one, the ugly one might just twist away from the motel and drag the bendy one away from the houses across the way as they fell . . . This was going to take a bit of working out.

I got over a couple of fences to have a look at the problem from another angle and I was bending down in someone's backyard, looking back between my legs at the top of the bendy tree to see how far out it was going to fall, when somebody started yelling inside the house that there was a prowler on the lawn. So I got out of there and put the headlight back in the Chadwick's car for them. Got it finished just in time before Alby arrived across with a breakfast tray for me. Very decent of the old bloke.

After Alby had cleaned up the breakfast dishes and done his housework I sent him off to hire a chainsaw. We had to run a jumper-lead from the battery out of the Hudson to get Alby's car started because their battery had gone flat during the night. Alby couldn't understand it because it was a practically new battery, but I reassured him that it'd come up all right with a bit of running and off he went.

He got back with the saw about an hour later but he hadn't brought any gas for it, so I siphoned some out of the Hudson into a tin and then drained some oil out of the sump into it until I had a near-enough two-stroke mixture. I found an axe-head I knew I had somewhere in the Hudson and Alby's gapped old *Plumb* was still in the toolshed where I'd spotted it the day before. So I got started.

As soon as I started the chainsaw there was a dirty great cloud of smoke. I'd been a trifle over-generous with the oil in the mixture, and it wasn't exactly the right oil for the job anyway, but it was too late to worry about that. I made my cuts

68

above the top of the fence because there was just a chance of one of the butt ends shooting back across the top of the stump, the way I had it figured. I scarfed the ugly tree a bit deeper than I dared and then put in a light back-cut, as far as I could tell through the smoke, angled to swing the fall away from the lean. I was hardly into the wood before the saw started dragging out brown dust instead of wood chips. She was rotten right through. Not a good sign.

Then I scarfed the bendy one, back-cut it till it started talking, and belted the axe-head into the motel side of the cut, using Alby's axe for a maul. And down they went. Just as some blokes arrived from the power board to save their wires.

I had a nasty moment when I heard the rotten crack of the ugly one breaking its holding wood clean, but both trees ended up lying along the right-of-way between the fences so I wasn't complaining. By this time half the district was standing around watching so I got a bunch of young fellers to throw the branches and blocks over the fence into the motel yard as I cut them off with the saw. And an hour later the job was done.

Alby rang up for a carrier to come and clean up the mess and I had lunch with the Chadwicks as though there'd never been any doubt about it. Alby was so pleased he wanted to pay me ten dollars, and I was so pleased I accepted.

After all, I'd done the job to get the trees out of his hair, not to save him money.

CHAPTER SEVEN
A GOOD KEEN GIRL

After lunch we were sitting around the Chadwicks' kitchen table yarning and I noticed that the daughter had been kind of looking at me for a while, and then out of the blue she said, "What sign of the Zodiac were you born under, Mr Hooper?"

"Don't think I'm a member," I told her.

And the old lady said, "Oh yes, Faith. *Do* Mr Hooper's horoscope!"

"That's all to do with the stars and stuff like that, isn't it?" I said.

"You'd be an Earth Sign, wouldn't you?" said the daughter.

"Every time,' I said. "Been on the land all my life."

"What's your date of birth?" she asked.

"August the twenty-sixth," I told her.

"What year were you born?" she wanted to know.

I worked it out and told her. She went a bit thoughtful on it.

"Is that good dear?" asked the old lady.

"Virgo," said the daughter. "I think Virgo and Capricorn are in sympathy just now. I'll get the *Almanac*."

She got up and went out of the room.

Alby got up and went out of the house.

The old lady reached over and grabbed me by the sleeve.

"Faith's got psychic perception, Mr Hooper," she said.

"Sorry to hear it," I said. "You want to get the local doctor to give her a going-over. It mightn't be as bad as you think.

How long has she had it?"

"No, no, Mr Hooper. You don't understand," said the old lady, pulling at my sleeve. "Faith can communicate with spirits from the Higher Astral Planes."

"That shouldn't be too tough these days," I said, "with this Commonwealth cable they're put in . . ."

Just then the daughter came in with a couple of books.

"What does it say, dear?" said the old lady.

The daughter looked something up in one of her books.

"Venus is in Capricorn and Virgo is in the Ascendancy," she said.

"How did they get there?" I asked, a bit confused.

"Our signs are compatible, Mr Hooper," said the daughter.

"Glad to hear it," was all I could think of to say.

"Here's yours," she went on, leafing through her book. "It says here that you are genial and persistent, good-natured and industrious, but liable to persecution if you were born after midnight. Your ruling planet is Mercury, disturber of our atmosphere (that means high winds and things), and your most fortunate day is Wednesday — that's today! You're a number-eight person and your fortunate gemstone is the sardonyx."

"Yeah?" I said.

"This is interesting," she went on, leafing again through the book. "Both our Planetary Configurations are very powerful at the Vernal Equinox, because the planets Mars, Uranus and Pluto are all within the orbs of a conjunction in the sign of Virgo and in the Twelfth House of the Ingress Map. Virgo, in conjunction with Venus, begins to move forward in space to join forces with Capricorn."

"It must be all these satellites they're sending up," I said. "There'll be a prang up there one of these days if they don't watch it."

"Here's Virgo," went on the daughter, leafing. "A Virgo should avoid animal foods as much as possible and live on fruits, herbs and vegetables. Wild carrot, wintergreen, ragwort, sage, plantain, shepherds purse, elderberry, gravel root, celery and angelica."

"*Ragwort?*"

"Yes. And it says here that you're prone to suffer from liver bile and intestinal disorders. Headaches, diseases of the blood, auto-poisoning and rheumatism."

"No wonder," I said. "*Ragwort!*"

"And the condition of the feet and lungs should be watched carefully," she added.

The old lady was looking at me as though I'd just felled a whole pine forest with a single fall-back, hang-up, tombstone or shattered log. "Isn't that wonderful!" she said.

"Doesn't sound too good to me," I said. "*Ragwort!* Have you ever seen what that stuff does to your cattle if they eat enough of it . . .?"

But the daughter had been leafing again. "Both our Affectional Associations are very auspicious just now. And it says right here in my horoscope that a man who will have a very strong romantic influence is about to come into my life."

They were both looking at me, so I said, "When's he supposed to be turning up?"

And then the carrier pulled into the yard with the head

gasket I'd been waiting for and put an end to the horoscoping for the time being.

I unwrapped the newspaper from around the gasket and saw right away that it was the right one, I also saw that it was pretty old and brittle. I paid the carrier and took my gasket over to the Hudson.

Alby came round to see if he could lend a hand but I wouldn't let him touch it. Secondhand head-gaskets are never terribly easy to work with and this one looked so delicate I didn't even like the idea of Alby watching.

And by the time I had three of the holes in the gasket fitted over three of the head studs it was broken in three places. The bit of newspaper it was wrapped in would have taken more punishment than that gasket. It was absolutely rotten.

Old Alby wasn't all that much help, either. When the thing was hanging on the studs in several different pieces he peered over my shoulder and said;

"It's not broken, is it?"

I tore the thing off and threw the three bits on the ground.

"It's euchred," I said. "I should have gone into town and got the thing personally. I'd have had her going again by now."

"Have you tried them at the garage along the road here?" said Alby helpfully. "They've got all sorts of spares."

I gave up on the idea of trying to explain to him what the odds were against the garage along the road having a cylinder-head gasket for a '36 Hudson straight-six. Instead I went in to use his phone again.

After nearly an hour of telephoning I gave up and went

outside to think, and I ran into Alby coming in the drive.

"Is this what you wanted?" he said holding up a brand new cylinder-head gasket for a '36 Hudson straight-six.

I snatched it off him to make sure it was real.

"Where did you get this?" I said.

"I took the broken one along to the garage down the road and they gave me that one. They said it belonged to a Dodge truck of some kind, but it's exactly the same as yours."

"It sure is," I said. "How much do I owe you?"

"Oh that's all right," he said. "Now that you've cut those trees down for us we can open the motel. It'd take a lot of head gaskets to pay you for that."

"It sure would," I couldn't help agreeing with him. "But we'll call it square at this, eh?"

I was so pleased with Alby that I let him help me slap the head back on the Hudson. It was a bit of a risk, letting him loose on a delicate piece of machinery like that, but the Hudson and I both survived it. We topped up the radiator and dipped a piece of rag into the petrol tank to squeeze into the throat of the carburettor. She started after a while and with a few minor adjustments I soon had her firing over as good as ever. I left her running for a while to warm up before giving her a final tighten-down.

By the time I'd gathered up all the tools and gear I had lying around it was time to go in and clean up for dinner. Alby wouldn't hear of me not eating with them, and since he was the cook I wasn't going to argue with him. I felt much better about things now I was mobile again.

I'd just come out of my unit to go across and have a beer

with Alby when the old lady intercepted me and plugged herself into my elbow.

"I just want to tell you how much we're enjoying having you here with us, Mr Hooper," she said confidentially. "Especially Faith. She's never been one to make a song and dance about things. She's the quiet type, really. A deep thinker. But since you've been here she's really started coming out of her shell."

"You could have fooled me," I said. "I thought she must have been shy of strangers, or something."

"Still waters run deep, Mr Hooper," said the old lady, giving my arm an extra squeeze. "It's not what people say, it's the *companionship* that counts. Don't you agree?"

"Too right," I agreed.

"And then there's your horoscopes. Isn't it wonderful having them compatible like that!"

"My oath," I said.

"It takes a lot to understand a girl like Faith, Mr Hooper," she went on. "But she'll make a wonderful little wife for some lucky man one of these days."

"Yeah, she looks like a good keen girl all right," I lied.

"There aren't many girls who have what it takes to put off getting married until they're sure they've found the right man. Faith's just over twenty-nine now, you know. Most young girls these days rush into marriage when they're hardly more than children. No wonder there are so many broken marriages. Thank goodness we'll never have to go through that with our Faith."

"Yeah," I said. "In fact it's a wonder she hasn't gone off before this. My mate Bert married his missus when she was

78

twenty, and they seem to hit it off okay. Bert reckon's it's because she's got maturity, and he ought to know."

"Faith's been waiting for the right man to come along," said the old lady, as though she hadn't been listening to what I'd said.

"Well let's hope he turns up soon or she'll be getting a bit long in the tooth on it," I joked.

"Faith will only do what she knows in her heart and mind is the right and proper thing, Mr Hooper," said the old lady seriously. "And of course she gets a lot of guidance from the stars, her having psychic perception and all. The number of times she's received warnings, you just wouldn't believe . . . "

And just then good old Alby waved a bottle of beer at me from the doorway and I went over to join him.

CHAPTER EIGHT
AFFECTIONAL
ASSOCIATIONS

"I'm thinking of getting married, Bert," I said. Bert lifted one side of his hat and slowly scratched above his ear, at the same time changing the foot he had on the second-from-bottom rail of the gate. Then he rubbed the back of his neck with his hand and left the front of his hat brim tipped down over his eyes, spat inscrutably past my arm, tilted his head back so he could look at me, and said: "Yeah?"

"Yeah," I said. "Later on in the year probably. I ran into her at this motel I stayed at. Her people run the place."

Bert absently took the watch out of the pouch on his belt and gave it a couple of thoughtful winds and buttoned it back into the pouch without looking at the time.

"What's she like?" he said.

"Seems all right. Reminds me a bit of that heifer of yours we pulled out of the drain down in the middle paddock last year. Kind of thin and dun-coloured to look at. Ordinary-looking, I suppose you'd call her. Name's Faith."

"How old?" said Bert, squinting down the barrel of his slasher and then digging at the toe of his gumboot with the end of the blade.

"She's about twenty-nine, far as I can remember."

"Sounds okay," said Bert noncommittally. "You'd better bring her out for us to have a look at, though. Betty'll want to check her over to make sure you haven't got yourself tied up with a crookie."

"She goes in for astrology," I warned him. "You know, all about the stars and that."

"What about it?" said Bert, lifting the gate up and down on the slack in its hinges a couple of times.

"I don't know. I just wondered if they usually — I mean I haven't taken much notice of them before and I was wondering if there's anything wrong with women who go in for astrology and stuff. What do you reckon? Do you think we ought to ask Betty about it?"

Bert thoughtfully ran his hat back and forth around his head and answered, "It's a perfectly natural thing with women, Kersey. You see, they have to have something psychological to fill the gap till their motherhood instincts are roused by childbirth."

I thought that one over for a moment.

"But do you think there's anything in it?" I said.

"Anything in it!" demanded Bert, throwing his slasher violently down into the mud at his feet. "Anything in it, you reckon? The bloody Egyptians had it all worked out thousands of years back, and you stand there and ask me if there's anything *in* it! They're just starting to realise how important it is. You've only got to pick up any newspaper, they're learning more about it every day. There's something in it all right, don't make any mistake about that little lot!"

"But she reckons it controls everything everyone does. A man's got no say in anything, it's all worked out for him from the moment he's born. I don't know, it all sounds a bit weird to me somehow."

Bert looked searchingly at my chest for a moment and then turned away as though he'd just remembered something urgent. When he'd gone about five yards he suddenly spun round again and strode right up to me and said:

"Kersey?"

"What?"

"We've been friends and neighbours now for — how long is it?"

"Going on four years," I told him.

"Going on four years," repeated Bert. "And in all that time, have you ever known me put you crook?"

"Not that I can think of," I said.

"And has Betty ever put you crook?" demanded Bert.

"No," I said, wondering what he was leading up to.

He turned away and back again with a big shrug, as though the whole thing had been made so clear a child could have seen it instantly.

"There, see!" he said.

"But Faith's never been on a farm in her life before," I said. "She mightn't want to stay here once she's seen the place."

In reply Bert held his open palm out in front of me and stabbed at it with the pointing-finger of his other hand. Then he said.

"Kersey?"

"What?"

"Had a farm hand once."

"Yeah?"

"Not a bad young bloke he was, either. The trouble was that

when he started with me he got whistling in the shed while we were milking. I figured it didn't matter all that much because it was going to take the cows a while to settle down with a stranger in the shed anyway. So I told him if he was going to whistle, whistle *all* the time or don't whistle at all. And he decided to whistle."

Bert paused to drape himself across the top rail of the gate and tip his hat right over the front of his face. He went on talking from behind the hat.

"Well, the cows were okay with this new bloke in the shed after a week or so. Turned out to be a good man with 'em. And he whistled all the time. Hardly noticed it in the finish."

"But what's that got to do with . . ." I started to say.

But Bert was holding up his hand. "Ah, ah, Kersey," he scolded. "That's the trouble with you. You're too impatient. Y'see, about six weeks before we were due to start drying off the herd for the winter, they came and collected my farm hand. Seemed he still had a bit of school work to catch up on before he was legally allowed to take a job. Young coot told me he was eighteen. Anyway I put the chains across the two end bails and milked 'em singlehanded after that. The whistling hadn't mattered up until then, but it mattered after they took the young bloke away. The cows had kind of got used to it, I suppose. Half of 'em wouldn't let their milk down unless I whistled to start them off, and whistling's a thing I've never been much good at. Used to finish the milking with my face all out of shape from whistling. Had to dry 'em off three weeks earlier than I expected."

"Still don't see what that's got to do with Faith not being

used to farming," I said.

"It's just this," said Bert, bending to pick his slasher out of the mud. "It's always better to get a farm hand who's never done it in his life before. That way you can train 'em the way you want. Once they've had a bit of experience they think they know everything, and it's bloody hard to bring 'em round to your way of doing things."

"I suppose you're right," I said dubiously.

"Too right I'm right!" said Bert grimly. "You just wait and see if I'm not."

During the months before the wedding there wasn't much time for romance because Faith and I only saw each other for a few hours once a week or so. But I had an idea that, even allowing for this, there ought to have been a bit more of this romance business tied up in it than just sitting next to each other and a hand-squeeze or a quick kiss on arrivals and departures.

Now that I had a woman of my own I was keen to try out all these capers people had been making such a fuss about. In fact I was actually toying with the idea of taking the initiative in certain experimental directions, at one stage. Fortunately I hinted as much to Bert in time to prevent something terrible from happening.

"You'd make it impossible for her to ever respect you if you did a thing like that, Kersey," said Bert accusingly.

I had to hand it to Bert. He might have been a bit slap-happy and unprogressive in his approach to farming, and he was a rotten judge of livestock, but when it came to handling women he certainly had me whacked. In fact I don't know how I'd have managed if it hadn't been for him and Betty.

"Blowed if I know, Bert," I told him. "I don't know how I'd have managed all this business with Faith if it hadn't been for you. I never knew there was so much in it."

Bert took his hat right off his head and meticulously re-formed the dent in the crown. Then he put it back on and turned to gaze humbly out across the river flats for a moment. Then, still looking out across the flats, he said:

"It's a matter of instinct, I suppose, Kersey. There's things some of us are just born with, and it's our responsibility to use this gift to help our fellow man whenever we can."

He turned to spread his arms in a gesture of appeal. "It's something that can't be put into words," he concluded.

The Chadwicks came out to the station a few times but they never got very far up the valley. In fact they never got past the woolshed. Once I offered to hook the sledge on to the tractor and take them up to the first river crossing, but they weren't very keen on the idea. They hung around the homestead mostly, making suggestions for how it was to be furnished and altered around. And they were usually pushed for time and had to get away.

Bert and Betty came over to meet them the second time they came. Betty snatched Bert's hat off his head in the porch as they came in and ruined the occasion for him somewhat. He leaned all over the mantelpiece looking uncomfortable, until Betty dragged him over to have Faith do his horoscope.

"What's your sign of the Zodiac, Bert?" Faith asked him.

"I don't think I've got one," confessed Bert. "You see, I came from a very large family and we couldn't afford that sort of thing. We lived too far out. No churches or anything for miles. . . ."

We all laughed and Faith spread her astrology books out on the kitchen table and worked out from his birthday that Bert was a Librian. Elegant and snobbish, loved company and was preoccupied with fashion. He was also inclined to a life of ease and pleasure and, if he was born in the late p.m., he would stop at little to indulge in these pleasures. Otherwise he was the happy possessor of a lovely nature, radiating goodness, and would be ideally suited for service in the ministry.

Bert went as red as a tractor and denied being anything like that, but Betty said it was him to a tee.

Betty, we discovered, was Aries. Intrepid and adventurous and headstrong, but with a very refined and humane disposition. If she was born after midnight she was very ardent and dynamic and attracted to and by the opposite sex. If she was born *before* midnight, however, she was less fortunate and apt to worry about self-injury and in danger of becoming a slave to her violent passions.

Betty said, "Oh dear."

And Bert announced that it was the best description he'd ever heard of her.

All in all everyone got along famously and it was the longest the Chadwicks stayed on any of their visits. After they'd gone Bert and Betty both pronounced that Faith was a hundred per cent, as far as they were concerned, and our union had their full approval. As a matter of fact I'm almost certain that the old lady had overheard Bert say to me:

"Grab this one, Kersey. She's a good keen girl!"

I would have preferred to have grabbed her in June, when things on the station would be fairly quiet, but Faith wouldn't hear of it. Her Planetary Regent was subjected to strong affectional opposition for most of June and July. And my Earth Sign moved in opposition to Mars, exerting critical separative trends. August the eleventh was the time when our Stellar Patterns were most beneficial and, as Betty pointed out, it was the most important day in a girl's life and I shouldn't mind a little bit of inconvenience. Like the lambing and calving.

Faith had a completely free hand in getting the house ready and I moved into the back bedroom. Bert explained how women don't value things in terms of what they cost in money, the way us men do. The truckload-and-a half of furniture and boxes and things they moved into the house cost me over seven hundred dollars.

I didn't mind the expense really because I'd been having a good run on the wild cattle, but I did get a bit of a shock when I saw what they were doing in the big bedroom. A big square double-bed with dark-stained shelves and cupboards attached to it, a wardrobe and dressingtable the same, and heavy red, purple, blue and bottle-green drapes and carpet. It was a bit overwhelming.

The whole house was getting uncomfortably cluttered and I was always nervous of knocking something over. I'd been given instructions not to touch a single thing unless Faith and Betty were there to supervise.

During the wedding plans I somehow got the impression

that the Chadwicks were feeling some kind of financial pinch, but they never said a word about it to me. In the finish I decided to find out.

"Are you people a bit hard up for money?" I asked them. "If you're feeling the pinch I'll kick in for the wedding expenses. I've got some money I'm not using at the moment."

But it turned out that I needn't have worried about it. Alby reassured me straight away.

"No, no, not at all," he said. "It's very kind of you to offer, but really we can manage, one way or another. Really!"

And the old lady said, "That's very sweet of you, Kersey dear, but we wouldn't dream of letting you . . . "

"Shut up," said Alby.

So we all shut up about it.

Three weeks before the wedding we all drove up to Seaforth to meet the vicar and have a rehearsal. Bert was my best man and Faith's off-sider was a cousin of hers who I hoped any kids we might have wouldn't throw towards. They had a couple of young girls to follow us around with flowers.

CHAPTER NINE
A GREAT START

I don't remember much about the actual wedding itself. All the men were sweltering in suits and the women in their hats looked like a bunch of frilly lead-head nails, fussing around her like a queen bee. You could hardly see Faith for a kind of wispy mutton-cloth she was draped in, but the old lady went round pulling at everyone's sleeve saying, "Doesn't our Faith look lovely!"

The bloke who done it gave a long talk about Heavenly Guidance that hadn't been in the dummy-run, and what with all the other bits and pieces the whole process took three or four times longer than I'd expected. Especially since we'd already been married once that day, down at the registry office.

Faith and I rode back to the motel for the wedding reception in a taxi that badly needed a valve-grind. We were to spend the first, and only, night of our honeymoon at the motel. Bert and Betty were staying on too, so we were all more or less stuck there.

I hardly saw Faith all evening. I'd had no idea she had so many relatives. My young brother and his wife were supposed to be coming over from Tarndale for the wedding breakfast but they didn't turn up. But Alby had got a fair bit of tucker and grog in and it wasn't too bad, once things got under way.

Some time during the evening Alby came up to me with his

hands and eyes wet from spilt champagne. His words were a bit wet too, I could feel them landing on the side of my face.

"The wife's out for my blood, Kersey," he confessed. "I'm not used to this kind of thing, you know."

"Neither am I," I assured him.

"I'm supposed to have a nice fatherly talk with you. Most important day in your life, you know. I can only tell you what I know from having been through exactly what you've got coming to you."

"What's that?" I asked him.

"The road ahead won't all be easy travelling. There'll be pitfalls. It seems only yesterday — and there she is, standing on the threshold — suddenly blossomed into womanhood."

"Where?" I said, looking around.

"Suddenly grown up and . . ."

He only got as far as that because just across the room Bert bowled up behind the old lady and slapped her on the rump and said in a loud voice:

"What in the blood and stomach pills do you think you're coming at, you muddy old bucket of pitch!" And then he roared with laughter, all on his own.

If you want to know why nobody would talk to Bert after that, just try saying, "What in blood and stomach pills do you think you're coming at, you muddy old bucket of pitch," out loud, and see what it sounds like.

Betty left the room in a shower of tears and Faith took off after her and they didn't come back.

Things started really breaking up after that and within three-quarters of an hour most of my new relatives had left. Bert bailed me up at the punchbowl and said, "The wife's out for my blood, Kersey. There was nothing wrong with what I said, was there? It was only a joke."

The upshot of Bert's little joke was that Betty and Faith slept in one motel unit and Bert and I slept in another — the one with the scratched bench in it.

Next morning Bert and Betty got away early, they'd already missed one milking. After breakfast I got the Hudson out while Faith was getting ready, and sat in it to wait for her. Alby was a bit crook and had gone back to bed, but a bit later the old lady came out and latched on to my sleeve through the car window.

"I'm so happy, Kersey dear," she said sniffling. "I just *know* that you and our Faith are going to be very happy together."

"Yeah, it should work out okay," I told her.

"You must remember that she's always been a city girl and be patient with her little mistakes and not expect too much of her all at once. She'll need time to adjust, especially with her sensitive nature. Remember that and I'm sure she'll be a loving and devoted little wife and companion for the rest of your lives."

"You don't want to let that worry you," I said, remembering what Bert had told me. "You get a lot of that sort of thing with farm hands. It's a sight easier to teach someone who doesn't know anything about farming, than to try and knock a bloke into shape who's done a bit of it and thinks he knows everything."

"Oh but this is different, dear," said the old lady. "This isn't a job Faith's going to, it's a whole new way of life. You see, it'll

97

all be strange to her, different from anything she's ever known. She'll need patience and understanding until she gets used to it. In other words you'll have to handle her very carefully at first."

"Yeah, I know what you mean," I told her. "It's the same when you're bringing in a heifer that's just calved for the first time. They're always a bit flighty at first, but they usually settle down after a while."

"Faith isn't a cow," said the old lady coldly, "and you'll find you can't treat her like one. She happens to be a young, sensitive, woman."

"Well I haven't had much experience with handling women," I said truthfully. "But if I run into anything I can't manage I can always ring Bert up. He's had a fair bit to do with 'em in his time. He had a bit of trouble with his own missus when he first got her, but he had her knocked into shape in no time at all. She's as good as gold now."

It was probably just as well that Faith turned up just then, carrying a couple of suitcases. There was a fair bit of nattering and weeping but eventually I got Faith and her suitcases loaded into the Hudson and we said goodbye all over again.

"Now don't forget what I told you," said the old lady to me as we took off.

I was so impatient to get away that I drove out on to the road a bit fast and almost hit a car that was coming. It was a pretty close shave and when I got the Hudson straightened up I looked across to see how Faith had taken it, but she didn't seem to have noticed.

"That would have been a great start, eh," I said.

"Don't be ridiculous," she said calmly. "We won't have any accidents today. It's a very good day for us. Venus is ascendant in Virgo and Jupiter's exerting a protective influence in my sign."

All the same, I drove carefully all the way home. I drove slowly up to the homestead to give Faith a good look at the road paddock. I'd put five hundredweight of cobaltised superphosphate to the acre on it a couple of months before and it was looking pretty good.

I don't mind admitting it, I was nervous that night.

I had a shave and got into my new pyjamas and waited at least half an hour after Faith had retired to the bedroom, as per Bert's instructions. Then I tiptoed along there, but I'd left it a bit too long and when I crept into the bedroom to sweep her off her feet she was already off them. She was fast asleep.

This was lovely. I sat on the edge of the bed for a while and coughed a few times. Then I staged an accident in which the *Day-to-Day Moon Guide* got knocked off the shelf by the bed. Then I got into the bed and had trouble getting comfortable. Then I got up again for a drink of water, turned out the light and stumbled against the foot of the bed on my way round to my side.

I lay there for a while and then decided to wind up the alarm clock. I reached out and tinkered with it, trying to find the winder. It had already been wound. There was a little bit of wind left in the alarm spring but it wasn't loud enough, so in a last desperate effort to stir up a bit of action and let her know that her lord and master had come to claim his conjugal rights,

I mucked around with the timing mechanism until the alarm accidentally went off. I had the thing ringing, right beside her ear practically, for several fumbling seconds, but it was no use. She didn't even stir. She must have been absolutely worn out to have slept through that lot.

So I gave up. I lay there in the dark wondering what might conceivably happen in the night to cause a terrific racket. Then she said, "Goodnight, dear," right beside my ear, and gave me such a terrific fright I had my arm round her before I could recover from my astonishment. And that gave me such a fright I pulled my arm away as though she'd been red hot.

I lay there, flat on my back with my arms by my sides, wondering what the hell Bert would have done in such a situation.

"What about kids?" I said a bit later, much too loud.

"Children?" she said.

"Yeah, do you feel like breeding or anything?"

"Oh I'm afraid that sort of thing is impossible," she said.

I sat bolt upright in the bed. "Impossible?"

"Yes," she said. "It's inauspicious," she added resignedly.

"Well do you think we ought to get it looked at," I suggested. "Sometimes these things can be fixed, can't they?"

"It's just that the time's inauspicious," she laughed. "Jupiter moves into Cancer tomorrow, and Scorpio is in descent with a critically disruptive force acting on Venus."

"Bastard," I said.

"It's no use swearing about it," said Faith. "Us Capricornians just have to put up with these sort of things. It's all very well for you tough old Virgos."

I didn't sleep too well that night. There seemed to be a strong disruptive force acting on my first impressions of married life. I was going to have to check with Bert on this little lot.

CHAPTER TEN
THE MISTRESS OF BLACKRANGE STATION

Right after breakfast next morning I went out to let the dogs off for a run. They'd been on the chain for a couple of days and were excited about me being back. I let them go and they jumped around me for a bit and then took off for a few circuits of the house, barking their heads off, like they usually did.

Then I heard a scream and a crash and the dogs came shooting round the side of the house and got in behind me with their hackles up. I ran round to see what had happened, and there was Faith. She'd been going to the rubbish hole in the yard with the scraps from breakfast in a big china bowl when the dogs had come belting round the corner and everyone got a fright. As soon as she saw the dogs with me she shrieked out for me to take them away and rushed inside and slammed the door.

They must have shook her up all right. Still, it wasn't their fault. They must have got a bit of a surprise themselves. I took them back to the kennels and chained them up and then went inside to comfort Faith. She was sitting in the kitchen blowing her nose.

"Did they give you a fright?" I said.

"They're horrid," she said, almost in tears, "They made me drop our nice big bowl."

"They always run around the house like that when they're let off the chain," I explained. "We'll get another bowl next time we go up to town."

"I'm not having those animals running around the house like that," she said.

She was obviously still pretty shaken up.

"It'll be okay when they get used to you," I said reassuringly. "In a couple of weeks you'll have them eating out of your hand. They reckon the best thing you can do in a case like this is go straight out and do it again. Otherwise you might be scared of dogs for the rest of your life."

"I've *been* scared of them *all* my life," she cried, "but never as scared as this. I never want to see the ugly things ever again."

And she ran into the bedroom and shut the door. Probably didn't want me to see her crying.

That afternoon we were going over to Bert and Betty's place for afternoon tea, so I did the lunch dishes while Faith got ready. I rustled up an old pair of gumboots for myself and gave Faith my good ones to wear. There's always quite a bit of mud around over at Bert's.

On the way up to their house I took Faith over and showed her the cowshed. We didn't waste much time there because she'd get a better idea of how it worked when they were doing the milking some time. I opened the yard gates so Bert could bring the cows straight in when he came down to get the shed ready and we headed on up to the house.

But poor old Faith. She got one of her gumboots stuck in the mud beyond the yards, and when she put the other gumboot forward to try and get some purchase, it got stuck too. And then, what with both feet stuck and her trying to turn back towards the concrete, she lost her balance. You should have seen her. Both feet stuck in gumboots half a dozen sizes too big for her, half turned round and bent over with both hands up to the wrists in mud. I was nearly over to her but the going just there was a bit heavy, even for me, and instead of waiting for me to give her a hand, guess what she does — she heaved on one leg and out it comes, out of the gumboot, and in it goes, into the mud, sock and all. I caught her just in time to save her tipping forward and sideways off balance. Just as well, too. If she'd gone right over we'd probably have had to take her back home and clean her up before we could carry on up to Bert and Betty's.

I lifted Faith out of the other gumboot and hoisted her up under one arm and carried her out through the mud and put her down on solid ground. She didn't weigh much more than a three-weeks-old bull calf. I showed her how to scrape most of the mud off with a splinter from a totara post and left her at it while I went back for her gumboots.

I had to hand it to Faith. Most town girls would probably have been put right off by what had happened. But she didn't utter one word of complaint. In fact I don't think she uttered a word of any kind at all. Come to think of it she just shoved her feet into those gumboots, mud and all, and squelched across the night paddock behind me towards the house.

By the time we'd got her cleaned up and fitted out with a pair of Betty's socks and had afternoon tea, it was time for them to bring the cows in. Faith didn't feel like helping with the milking that day, so on the way home I showed her how to open and close Taranaki gates, and pointed out some of our boundaries to her.

The day's activities had taken more out of her than I'd thought. She couldn't even be bothered making us a cup of tea when we got back to the house. She just dragged herself off to the bathroom and ran a bath. She was still in it at dinner time, so I made us a hash. Faith decided to have hers in bed, and when I went in to see how she was getting on she was fast asleep, with her hash hardly touched.

Betty and Faith were good mates, which was a good thing, seeing as they were the only two women for miles, but the sad thing about it was that every time Faith went near Bert's place she ran into trouble. She couldn't open the gates and there were only a few places she could get through Bert's fences.

The first thing she ran into was Bert's old house-cow, Maude, standing on the other side of the only place Faith could get into the paddock. They stood there looking at each other.

"Shoo," said Faith.

Maude blinked slowly and then flicked her tongue up one nostril, then the other, dropped her gaze and went on chewing her cud as though the interview was over.

Faith went back to the cowshed paddock and had a go at getting through to Betty's house that way. She'd just crawled through the fence into the calf paddock when the calves cantered up and took her basket off her. They must have thought it was a bucket of milk. They trod the basket and its contents into the mud. Faith came running home in tears.

Bert's bull bellowed at her, his horse snorted at her, his dog barked and sniffed at her, and one of his pigs finally did the trick. She'd been trying to walk around the mud in Bert's road paddock and ended up right across the other side. The sow must have thought Faith was playing when she backed away along the fence, and it ended up chasing her across the paddock, with Faith yelling her head off. The pig probably wouldn't have chased after her at all, but she was running in the direction of the pigsty and it was getting on towards the time when Betty usually went down to feed them.

Betty came down and saved her in the finish, but Faith wouldn't go near Bert's place after that and Betty had to do all the visiting.

But it wasn't only Bert's animals who Faith didn't hit it off with. I don't know, but whenever she went near an animal it would do something either frightening or embarrassing. I tried to explain to her that it was probably because she was so nervous of them and they could tell, but it was no use. She couldn't even collect the eggs because the first time she went down to the fowl-house Biddy, the old Orpington, wouldn't get off the nest. Faith waited for her to move for quite a long time, and then she got impatient and said, "Oh you stupid hen," and gave Biddy a fright. She exploded off the nest in a squawking flurry of feathers and gave Faith such a scare she wouldn't go near the fowlrun except to throw food to them after that.

The one thing she would have got on all right with, perhaps, was the sheep. They would have run away from her and left her alone, but she never gave them the chance to show her.

It was a bit of a knock-back to me, Faith being so nervous of animals. Even our own dogs barked at her as though she was a stranger. But Bert, with his hat clinging precariously to one side of his head, trod a drain in the mud to let the water out of one puddle into the next and said:

"You've got to remember that town people haven't had the same privileges as us, who've been brought up amongst animals all our lives, Kersey. Just think how long it'd take you to get used to working in an office."

Herepo bounced in through the gateway on his old Ferguson one afternoon to get his old job back again, with a new dog running along behind on a long rope. I could see straight away, by the look on his face, that he knew I was married.

"G'day, Herepo," I said. "I suppose you want your old job back again."

"The boss told us . . ."

"Yeah yeah. Just put your gear in the shed there in the meantime until we get a bunk sorted out for you."

Herepo paused cunningly with his sack of personal belongings half-unlashed from the defunct three-point hydraulic linkage on his tractor and said,

"I hear the little miromiro has visited you, boss."

"What are you talking about?"

"The miromiro, boss. The little messenger of love. You get the good wahine, eh!"

"Mind your own bloody business," I said. "You'll see her for yourself soon enough."

Herepo and Faith were at loggerheads from the very start. I

110

think Herepo probably kicked it off by digging Faith in the apron with his broken old fingernail and saying,

"Nothing in the oven yet, eh missus?"

And as Faith backed away he said seriously,

"If you want the baby you get your old man to find a big old hinau tree for you. You put your arms round the body of the tree, like this. The side where the rising sun strikes the hinau is the side for a boy. And the side were the setting sun strikes the tree is the side for a girl. If you want a girl," he added, as though there was something wrong with her if she did prefer a girl.

"We're planning our family by the stars," said Faith coldly. "Not by some tree or other."

"Ah," said Herepo, blissfully unaware that he was treading on dangerous ground. "Whanau-marama. The children of light."

"I'm talking about the stars and planets," said Faith. "The ones up in the sky. I don't suppose you even know what star sign you are. Probably late Aries, by the look of you."

"I don't belong to the stars, missus. Only the children of Maunganui can be stars. The Maori believes that Tane brought the children of Marama from Maunganui in the big basket of the Milky Way and threw them on the blue robe of Rangi the Sky Father to make him beautiful," said Herepo.

"Yes, well we're a little more advanced than that," said Faith. "We're more scientific about it."

"Us horis aren't scientific, missus," said Herepo. "We believe what our fathers tell us of the stars. The old Maoris used to say that when Tawhaki walks the skies . . ."

111

At this point I left them to it and went down to the yards to have a look at a footrot ram I'd drafted out of the mob that morning. And when I went back to the house Faith was drumming her fingers on the table while old Herepo told her about a bloke called Rona who went crook at the moon one night and the moon swooped down and grabbed him. Rona grabbed hold of a ngaio bush and hung on, but the moon heaved and Rona got taken up into the sky. You can see him up there in the moon sometimes, Herepo reckoned, still hanging on to his uprooted ngaio bush.

A few nights later as we got into bed Faith said, "Really, Kersey, that Maori! I don't know why we have to put up with him,"

"Herepo? Why, what's wrong with him?"

"He's primitive," said Faith. "He tried to tell me today that the Pleiades in Taurus are the left eyes of seven great chiefs. And he thinks meteors and falling stars are children falling off his sky-god's cloak. It's ridiculous!"

"No more ridiculous than . . ." I nearly said.

"No more ridiculous than *what?*" Faith wanted to know in her no-uncertain-terms voice.

"I suppose it is a bit ridiculous when you come to think of it," I said.

"How much longer are we going to have to put up with him?" said Faith. "He doesn't seem to do very much work for you."

"Herepo's going over to Bert's the day after tomorrow to give Bert a hand with some concreting," I told her. "He'll probably take off for his brother-in-law's place after that. He never stays around here once the lambing starts."

And I was right. Herepo drove up to the implement shed a couple of days later and started helping himself to a few gallons of petrol out of my drum. I went over to make sure he didn't overdo it.

"You off again, Herepo?" I said.

"Yes, boss. Every year at this time I go to help my brother-in-law with the kumaras."

"But you never went till a fair bit later than this last year," I pointed out.

"I know, boss," he said. "But this year the planting season is early. Atutahi has been in the sky for a few nights now, and this morning I heard the first cuckoos. That tells me, 'Herepo, it's time to go and help with the kumaras.' So I go."

And thus the koekoea spread his crafty old wings and migrated to the warmer climes of his brother-in-law's kumara patch, just as the first lambs of the season bleated across the scrubby Blackrange hillsides.

CHAPTER ELEVEN
CRITICAL TRENDS

I was re-gulleting a fishtail peg-and-drag crosscut saw in the implement shed one day when Bert wandered in.

"How's she going, Kersey?"

"How's what going?"

"Well, how's married life treating you?"

"Good."

"Good."

I went on with re-gulleting the saw. Bert watched for a while. Then he said, "Well I'll let you get on with it. See you later."

"Bert," I said.

He stopped in the doorway, "What?"

"Have much trouble with sex when you first got your missus?" I asked.

Bert walked slowly back with his lips grimly pursed and put one hand on the bench beside me to balance himself while he hooked one of his gumboots off on the toe of the other. Then he pulled a piece of cocksfoot out of his sock, pulled the sock on to his foot properly, put his foot back into the gumboot and stamped on the floor a couple of times to make sure it was on properly.

"Too right," he said, straightening up and adjusting his hat. "You always get a bit of that."

"How long does it take 'em to come right?" I said.

Bert stood silently shaking his head from side to side and then he picked up the file I'd been using and rapped sharply on the bench with it.

"It all depends," he said.

"Depends on what?"

"Sometimes they come right, and sometimes they don't," said Bert, poking me in the stomach with the end of the file to emphasise each word. "And when they come right there's no guarantee they're going to stay that way."

"How do you tell when they *have* come right?"

"They'll let you know soon enough," said Bert. "Don't make any mistake about that little lot. But you've got to be careful," he said.

"Careful?"

"Yeah, bloody careful."

"How do you mean?"

Bert bent and ran the file expertly across the face of a tooth on my good fishtail peg-and-drag, completely taking the angle off both that tooth and the one next to it. I reached out and took the file off him.

"How do you mean, you've got to be careful?" I insisted.

"Well," said Bert, "it's like this. One day you can bowl in and knock 'em over like a yearling bull, and they're all for it. But try the same caper next time and you'll find yourself out on the sofa before you know what's happened. There's been a lot of time and hard thinking put in on that one over the years, but no one's come up with the reason for it yet, not as far as I know."

"They're not like cows or anything, are they?" I asked.

"I wouldn't know anything about that," said Bert quickly.

"I mean once a year or something," I explained.

"Nothing as clear-cut as that," said Bert. "But there's times I begin to wonder."

"What about dogs, every few months?"

"No, nothing like it. Just as well, too, come to think of it. It's bad enough as it is sometimes."

"Well how the hell is it?" I asked him.

Bert paused to go over and get a billhook out of the corner and bring it back to lean on.

"Y'see, Kersey, women aren't the same as us. They're built different, for a starter."

"In what way?"

Bert looked at me. "You ought to have found *that* out by now," he said.

He paused again, this time to get a hole started in my implement shed floor with the end of the billhook.

"Sex is funny stuff, Kersey. The more you get, the more you get. And the less you get, the less you get. It's a big thing when you look into it."

"Look into it?"

"Yeah, it's been going on since time immemorial. Take that Roman sheila, for example, Cleopatra. Caused no end of trouble between a couple of them Roman generals. They got a war going over it in the finish. Lasted for donkey's years, so I believe. Thousands of jokers ended up getting knocked off. And all because this bloke's missus jumped the fence on him one night and clambered into the sack with the bloke who ran the army across the border."

119

"What happened to her?"

"I don't remember exactly what happened to her," said Bert, "but that's not the point. Look what happened to all them Roman soldiers. You'd never catch me volunteering to join up and fight for that Elizabeth Taylor sheila, you can put a ring around that lot. I'd turn conchy first," he concluded indignantly.

Just then Faith appeared in the doorway of the shed to tell us lunch was ready. But nothing would persuade Bert to stay for a feed. It was as though he'd just found out someone had left all his gates open. He was very anxious to get back to his place and we didn't see him for several days after that.

Faith had quite a few accidents with the cooking at first. It was probably because she wasn't used to the stove. In fact she never really did manage to get the knack of handling it properly. I'd never been very fussy about food so I didn't particularly mind it when the meat was a bit black or red, or both, though I did have a sneaking preference for the undercooked rather than the overcooked vegetables. It wasn't long before I got used to both though.

Faith herself wasn't so fortunate. Some of the stuff I could eat without turning a hair was more than her delicate Capricornian system could cope with. Our star signs might have been compatible but our stomachs weren't. She needed things like onions, garlic, horse radish, leeks, rhubarb, wormwood, spearwort, betony and ginger, and quite often she would have to tip her whole meal into the fowl scraps and have scrambled eggs on toast instead.

But the bathroom. That was a different matter all together. I couldn't cope with the bathroom. For a start there was a big orange woolly bath-mat on the floor that I was never quite sure whether to stand on or not. And there were rubber hats and fancy towels and face-cloths and stockings and stuff like that strung up all over the place in there. There were bottles and jars and tubes and creams and cakes and boxes and bags. There were things made of wire and wood and cardboard and glass. There were plastic and foam-rubber hair-curlers, and a pink plastic hair-dryer that whined like a generator, though she woke up every morning with her hair like a handful of hay. There were tools and trays and clippers and files. And a big spongy thing on the end of a curved wooden handle. Eyebrow tweezers and eyelash curlers and a fine steel comb for dandruff. There were jars of cleansing creams, bubble baths and astringents. There were medicines and pills and ointments and powders and tonics and conditioners, not to mention aerosol cans, pumps, brushes and roll-ons. The whole bathroom looked like the top of the dressingtable in the bedroom.

I'd seen that sort of stuff piled up in the windows of chemists' shops, but to come face to face with it in my own bathroom was a bit overwhelming.

Faith spent long times in the bathroom, which was so cluttered with all these strange things that I was nervous of even going in there, in case I accidentally upset something. I washed up mostly in the wash-house, and the bathroom got to be Faith's part of the house almost exclusively.

"I don't know, Bert," I said to him, "but Faith's skin must be in a pretty bad way for her to need all that kind of stuff. Do you think she might have some kind of disease or something?"

Bert stood at the fence with one leg forward and the other one back, as though stopped in mid-stride, with his hands shoved down the front of his trousers and his thumbs hooked over his belt-buckle, squinting grimly into the distance as though he was too preoccupied to have heard what I'd said. Then he spoke:

"Us men just don't know what our women have to go through, Kersey," he said.

"But there might be something bad wrong with her."

"Let's put it this way," said Bert, "What do you do if your soil's got a deficiency?"

"You get 'em to test it."

"Right! And what do you do if they find out it needs phosphate? Do you walk off the farm?"

"No," I said. "You slap on the fertiliser."

"Well that's how it is with skin," said Bert with a triumphant sweep of his arm towards the house.

"I wonder if she's using the right sort of stuff, though," I said. "I suppose she must be, considering the range and amount of it she's got."

We'd been married for over five weeks and this time it was:

"No, Kersey dear. Not tonight. Not while Jupiter's in my Sun Sign. The trends are too critical and separative."

And that's how it had been going ever since we'd got married. If the sun wasn't in detriment, Jupiter would have moved into my Solar House, or some other disruptive factors would be at work, like Mars forming a trine to Jupiter and, along with Saturn's restrictive influence, would be causing strong Planetary Conflicts of one sort or another,

This was no good to me. I decided to try a few separative trends of my own. I moved into my old back bedroom without saying a word to Faith about it, and when she asked me why, I was going to tell her. That'd fix her.

But she didn't ask. The first night I slept on my own she just asked me in the morning if I'd been comfortable, and all I could say was, yes, I had been. She didn't even mention it after the second night, and on the third night I realised I'd have to take positive drastic action.

I went to bed straight after dinner to make it even more unusual and remarkable, but she didn't remark. I had to lay there listening to her moving about the house because it was too early to sleep. She must have been worried about me though. I heard her go to bed at the usual time and read for a while. Then she turned out her light. I lay there listening to how upset she was, and she was upset all right. She was so upset she didn't make a sound. She was pretending to be asleep.

I didn't want her to worry about me not being warm enough, on top of everything else, so I decided to creep in and get the blanket off the foot of the big bed. Then she'd be able to resign herself to the fact that I had no intention whatsoever of coming to bed with her and she'd be able to get off to sleep,

She'd left the bedroom door slightly open and I accidentally knocked it back against the shelf by the bed on my way into the room, but she was pretending to be so asleep by this time that she didn't even stir. I had to fumble around the foot of the bed in the dark to get the blanket which was folded across the foot of it, and I was just making for the door with it when Faith sat up and screamed.

I screamed.

Faith screamed.

"Shhhhh!" I said.

She screamed again. "It's all right, it's me, Kersey," I said. She screamed again.

I got the light turned on and as soon as I got her quietened I had to go out and quieten the dogs down. They were barking their heads off. I trod in something out by the gate and had to wash my feet before I went back into the house, and by this time Faith was calling out for me, so I made a cup of tea and took it into her, but when I was halfway along to the bedroom the generating plant out in the shed ran out of diesel and all the lights went out.

Faith screamed. I spilt tea all over the place getting in to her and after a while I got a candle lit and quietened her down again. She was pretty worked up by this time and I couldn't very well let her sleep all on her own in that state, so I didn't.

And it was a couple of nights after that when Neptune exerted a favouring influence in Capricorn and there was a Beneficial Vibration from Mars in Virgo.

"What about if you want to put off having any kids so you can arrange it that they're born in February, Bert?" I asked him.

Bert put both hands over his face and stood like that until he almost went off-balance. Then he took off his hat and carefully reshaped the tilt of the brim, then he put it back on his head and said:

"Why?"

"Why what?"

"What's on in February?" he wanted to know.

"Nothing really," I explained. "It's just that if we *are* going to have kids Faith wants the first one to be born under the sign of Aquarius. It's this astrology stuff she's keen on. She takes it pretty seriously, you know. It doesn't matter two hoots to me, but if it keeps her happy I don't mind going along with it."

"Yeah?"

"Yeah. All I want to know is the best way of organising it."

"Well there's all sorts of ways," said Bert. "But the only dead-sure way is to put the whole thing off until you want to start breeding, but I've even seen *that* fail."

"Eh?" I said.

"Tell you what," said Bert. "I'll get Betty to have a yarn with Faith about it. She'll put her right. Us blokes aren't much good at that sort of thing."

And when Betty came over next day to get their half of a sheep Bert and I had killed the day before, she took Faith into the house for a chat. I wasn't invited so I worked handy to the house in case they wanted to let me know how they were getting on. And about an hour later Betty came out and as she went past me she said, "Now you look after the little lady, Kersey, or you'll have me to deal with, I'm just off to get the shed ready. Bert's been working up on the Tiltons' boundary today so he'll bring the cows in with him when he comes. And you know what he's like about his cup of tea, he won't start the milking without it, bless his heart. So I'd better get along."

I went in and asked Faith if there was anything wrong, but there didn't seem to be, so I decided to leave the whole thing to her. I had plenty to keep me occupied without having to worry about that anyway.

The year ended with me being very busy trying to catch up on a few of the things I hadn't been able to get done on the station. What with getting ready to get married, getting married, and then being married, I hadn't got much work done that season.

But, as Bert pointed out, a man's got to make a few adjustments at first and it all takes time. There'd be plenty of time to catch up on the work once Faith and I were properly run-in, so to speak.

CHAPTER TWELVE
VERY UNPLEASANT

At Christmas time we spent a whole month with the Chadwicks at the motel, or rather one of us did. Faith went as cold as the set of chisels I'd bought her for Christmas and after three days I decided to have to get back to the station to take care of some urgent business that needed attending to. I didn't get back to the motel to pick up Faith until towards the end of January, but I took Sneak with me for the ride.

And I was just being greeted at the door by the Chadwicks when suddenly their Siamese cat shot hissing and bristling out from behind one of the motel units and into the house past us, with Sneak flat-out after it. They scrabbled and scratched across some linoleum in the kitchen and disappeared up the hall. The chase ended in the old folks' bedroom with the cat hissing and prowing halfway up the curtains and Sneak leaping and barking at it.

There was nothing to throw or lash out with so I had to kick Sneak down the passage and out of the house, and tie him to the bumper with a length of rope out of the Hudson.

"He's been getting stuck into the odd possum round the homestead," I explained to the Chadwicks.

I slept in one of the motel units that night, they always seemed to put me in the one with the scratched bench. In the night Sneak chewed through his rope and dug a few holes in the lawn and flower garden. Then he scattered the contents of the rubbish tin around a bit and jumped in through the laundry window, chewed the old lady's kangaroo-skin handbag and everything in it to shreds, chewed the tongues out of Alby's slippers, and then made himself comfortable in a pile of clean washing in Alby's ironing basket, where Alby found him in the morning, sound asleep after his night's labours. I had to poke him out from under the old lady's bed with a broom.

"He's not used to town life," I explained to them. But it wasn't too hard to see that this explanation was somewhat less than satisfactory.

We all agreed that it was unthinkable to expect Faith to ride all the way back to the station with that dog in the car, and since it was equally unthinkable to leave him behind, it was agreed that Sneak and I would have to go back on our own and I could return for Faith in a day or two.

While all this was going on Sneak had gone down to introduce himself to the neighbour's fowls, but judging by the uproar they'd apparently misinterpreted his intentions and panicked. He came slinking back and got in under the Hudson, and when I went to poke him out I discovered he'd been rolling in something rotten, so I had to get the hose out and wash him. By the time I drove away that day things with the Chadwicks were very bleak indeed.

I told Bert all about it when I got back to the station.

"I don't know, Bert," I said. "But every time I go to town things go haywire on me."

"They sure do," agreed Bert.

It wasn't until a few weeks later that I was able to return, on my own this time, to collect Faith.

130

I'd put in some good burns while Faith was away and all the way up the valley the manuka and second growth and shingle slides lay against the hillsides in big wedge-shaped strips, with the faint green of new fern and grass already coming away on the burns along the leading ridge tops. The sheep were black from feeding amongst the burnt manuka. The cattle were doing well and I was looking forward to a good season.

But Faith received one of her warnings and consulted the Planetary Configurations and announced that the square of Venus to Saturn pointed to a number of sadistic murders of women and would also bring some very unpleasant weather conditions, which would interfere with sporting arrangements in the coming year.

Part of what she said was certainly right. The bit about the very unpleasant weather conditions. It was the worst seasons for floods the district had seen for years.

I spent nearly three weeks splitting posts and strainers and battens out of four dead totara logs on the crest of a ridge high above the river an hour's ride up the valley. Got 453 posts, 19 strainers, 270 battens and sundry stays and blocks. I shot them all down across the valley to the other side of the river on a long wire and before I could shift them it rained and the river flooded.

I saved 82 posts and 11 battens and all the strainers. The rest got washed out to sea and became hazards to shipping until they were washed up on the rocks along the coast. Bert ended up with quite a few of them on his place.

During one of the worst floods, Herepo drove up with both feet on the brake pedals of his Fergy, clutching the steering wheel for more purchase, and ran into my yard fence to bring the thing to a stop.

"Why the hell don't you get those bloody brakes of yours done up, Herepo?" I said to him. "One of these days you'll either wreck something you can't pay for, or you'll have a prang and kill yourself."

"She's right, boss," said Herepo. "They mostly get out of the way when they see me coming."

"Yeah, I don't blame 'em," I said. "But how are they to know you've got no brakes?"

"It's easy, boss," he said. "When a car comes up the road or somebody's in the way I swerve the tractor across the road a few times. All over the place. They give me plenty of room all right."

"They probably think you're drunk."

"It works, all the same," said Herepo unanswerably.

He travelled some great mileages on his old tractor, hundreds of miles, over some pretty steep and winding roads, too. He must have had it worked out to a pretty fine art.

"I suppose you want your old job back again?" I said.

"No, boss," said Herepo. "I just called in to see you. I'm on my way past to my brother-in-law's house. Te Ihorangi won't let you get much work done round here this year, boss. He picks on this place."

"Who the hell's Ihorangi?"

"Rain, boss. Te Ihorangi is the tears of Rangi, the Sky Father, crying for the Earth Mother. And I think Te Ihorangi will give you a bad time this year, boss."

"How do you make that out?" I said, waving his attention

132

towards the brown floodwaters that filled the Blackrange Valley from hill to hill.

"Atutahi, boss," said Herepo. "The Maori says that when Atutahi appears in the south at the time for planting the kumara, his light should shine towards the north. That means a warm fine season for growing. But this time Atutahi's rays shone towards the south. That means there will be a lot of rain and snow."

"And just what *is* this Atutahi?" I asked him.

"Atutahi is the star that jumped out of Tane's basket, boss. You can see him at night, all by his own. He comes up over that ridge there," he said pointing. "Te Ihorangi will give you a bad time this year, all right, boss."

And Herepo was right. The worst floods were yet to come.

It was a long winter and I only had to saddle the mare and start riding up the valley for Ihorangi to start crying again. The pump shed, ten feet above flood level, got washed away. A slip carried several chain of new fence off the side of the hill and eight of my cattle got away into the bush. I had a hell of a job finding them and bringing them back. I only got twelve head of wild cattle that year, too. Partly because of Ihorangi and partly because Sneak was getting old and cunning and lazy.

I had to lend Bert some of my hay to carry him through the winter, and then ran out of it myself and had to buy more in at more than I could afford. I only had sixty head of stock worth sending away that year, and although I managed to shear five hundred sheep the wool prices were lower than they had been for years. I had to sell off seventy-five wether hoggets to keep the place going.

Eleven sheets of iron blew off the woolshed roof in a storm and we had to keep candles and lamps ready in the house at all times because the lighting plant was becoming unreliable and I didn't have time to fix it.

If the weather gave me a rough time that year, the Stellar Patterns gave me an even rougher one. My good keen girl was enduring the very unpleasant weather conditions as though she'd been expecting them, and she even began to take an interest in the running of the station, if it could be called that. You see, everything had to be done by the stars. I didn't like to knock Faith back because I'd been pretty anxious to see her show an interest in the place outside the house.

But the planting and sowing had to be done by the moon's phases and these clashed with the very unpleasant weather conditions almost every time. In short, our vegetable garden was a complete washout.

Wild pork had always been a useful source of food on the station, but we discovered that pigs could only be killed between five and ten in the morning and between the first quarter and the full moon, which, along with the very unpleasant weather conditions and all the other things I had to do, severely restricted my activities in this department. And right when I should have been docking the lambs the moon moved through three Critically Adverse Signs for castration and I was two months late getting some of them done.

And the dogs still weren't allowed inside the house yard.

CHAPTER THIRTEEN
Psychology Versus Astrology

All this astrology stuff of Faith's was getting a bit ripe. In fact I was so concerned about it I decided to ask Alby what to do. He'd lived with it for years and might be able to give me a few clues, so I got him on the phone when Faith was out of the house one afternoon.

"What about this astrology business of Faith's, Alby?" I asked him.

"What about it?" he said.

"Well what do you do about it? I mean, how do you put up with it?"

"I don't have to now," he pointed out.

"But what *did* you do about it?"

"Walk out and leave 'em to it," said Alby.

It would have been even less use asking the old lady about it, so I decided to ask Bert next time I saw him.

"I tell you, Bert," I said. "The situation's getting desperate."

"It usually is around this time of year," said Bert.

"It's not *that* I'm worried about so much," I said. "I can handle that. It's this blasted astrology of Faith's. If she goes on running the place by the stars it'll ruin me. It's worse than an outbreak of foot-and-mouth."

"Why don't you tell her to cut it out?" said Bert.

"I can't," I told him. "She thinks I believe in the stuff now."

"Well *do* you believe in it?"

"Hell no, I couldn't afford to, even if I wanted to. The trouble is I thought it'd encourage Faith to take an interest in the station if I let her advise me by the stars. And now I'm sort of stuck with it. Hell, Bert, I can't even keep my bull because he's been turning out the wrong-coloured calves. What's a man to do?"

Bert suddenly walked away along the fence, but he was only going to get the horse that was tied to the rails and bring it along to where we were, so he could lean on it. He tied it to the fence and slapped it on the neck.

"There's only one answer, Kersey," he said grimly.

"What's that?"

"If you can't beat 'em, join 'em."

"How do you mean?"

Bert spent a few moments examining one of the stirrup leathers on my saddle, then he tested the girth and tightened it up a hole.

"It's simple," he said. "You're going to have to use the psychological approach. Beat her at her own game. You'll have to pretend to be terribly interested in astrology yourself. More interested than she is. Don't talk about anything except astrology, and before you know where you are she'll have had a proper gutful of it."

"You think so?"

"Bloody sure of it," said Bert definitely. "It's psychological, it can't fail."

"But I wouldn't know how to go about it," I protested.

"Well find out," said Bert. "There's bound to be plenty of background stuff in those books of Faith's. All you have to do is swot up on it a bit, on the side, like, so she doesn't twig what you're up to."

I had to admit that Bert's idea seemed pretty good.

The more I thought about it the better it looked. So I sneaked an old book of Faith's out of the house and hid it in the woolshed to study up on whenever I got a bit of time to spare. Actually it meant I had to neglect my work a bit, but the end result would be well and truly worth it, if it worked.

The things I found in that astrology book were a bit confusing at first. I hadn't realised there was so much in it. But by the time I'd been at it for a couple of weeks I was ready to put the scheme into action. I'd learnt up enough star-stuff to out-astrology Faith, I reckoned, and I was looking forward to having a go at it. I got my chance after breakfast one morning.

"When are you going to dig the new rubbish hole for me, Kersey?" said Faith. "You know the old one's been full for days now. It's starting to pile up and the smell's something awful."

"I'd like to have done it today for you," I said regretfully. "But I'm afraid it's impossible."

"Why, is there something wrong out the back?" she said.

"No, everything's okay out the back," I said.

I had her guessing now!

"Well why can't you dig a new rubbish hole today?" she asked.

"Because Mars is in opposition to Neptune and Virgo in conjunction with Uranus begins to move backward in space from nineteen thirty-six to sixteen thirty-seven," I said.

"But . . ." she started to say. But I stopped her. (Might as well give her the works good and proper while I was at it.)

"Not only that," I went on, "but the sun enters Libra on the twenty-third at six-eighteen p.m. and Virgo's influence is intensified by the Sextile Aspect of Jupiter from Gemini and I'm not digging any bloody rubbish hole as long as Pluto stays in the Eleventh House."

"Nonsense," said Faith.

"And not only that," I went on again, "but Mercury's in retrograde motion and the principal aspects of the third quarter are unauspiciously critical."

"Rubbish," said Faith. "You don't know what you're talking about."

But I was fighting for the Blackrange Station by this time and I wasn't going to be put off that easily.

"Jupiter moves into my Solar House in the spring quarter," I said.

"What nonsense," said Faith. "Jupiter happens to be . . ."

"The sun entered Aries on the twenty-fifth of March last year at eight-twelve p.m. Greenwich Mean Time!" I shouted desperately. I was running out of material.

"Oh don't be so ridiculous, Kersey," she said. "If you don't want to dig a rubbish hole I'll just have to ask Bert to do it for me. As far as your stars are concerned Jupiter happens to have moved into your Solar House yesterday morning, exerting a protective influence, and you're already receiving help from Venus. And as for all that nonsense about Mars and Neptune . . ."

"All right, I'll dig your bloody rubbish hole," I said. I know when I'm licked.

When I told Bert what had happened he shoved his hands deep into the pockets of his old oilskin and paced back and forth for a while as though he was in a cell. Then he turned on me as though I'd let the whole side down very badly, and said:

"I told you to *beat* her at her own game, Kersey. Not try and *bluff* her at it. After all, she's the expert. Only a mug would have . . . "

"Yeah, yeah," I said. "I can see all that. The thing is, what am I going to do now? My whole way of life is being jeopardised by this bloody astrology. It could even cost me the station if it goes on much longer. I mean — what would you do in my position?"

Bert had to think about that one.

"I wouldn't *get* into your position," he said. "Not for all the tea in China," he added.

"But what would you do if you were?" I said. "I can't put up with it much longer."

"Well, don't."

"Don't what?"

"Don't put up with it."

"How do you mean?"

"You're going to have to put your foot down, Kersey, whether you like it or not. Make her get rid of all her astrology books and things and tell her the subject's never to be mentioned in your house again. It's the only way. She'll have a lot more respect for you if you do that. You've got to stick up for your rights, you know."

Bert was right. I'd been too easy-going about Faith and her astrology. I knew exactly what to do, but it would have helped considerably if I'd known how to do it.

After dinner that night I said, "Faith."

"Yes, dear?"

"This astrology business," I said. "It's all very well and I'm not saying there's nothing in it. It might be very good in some circumstances, but when it comes to running a sheep and cattle station it's just not what it's cracked up to be."

"Yes, dear?"

"So I want you to put all your astrology books and charts away and leave them there. For a while," I added because she was looking at me as though I was telling her a particularly dirty joke.

Then she burst into tears and ran to the bedroom and slammed the door. She stayed in bed for two days, by the end of which time I was feeling such a rotten bastard I was quite happy to drop the subject of astrology and putting my foot down for the time being. There must be other ways.

There *were* other ways, but none of them worked. I'll never forget the time I finally did do my block. Faith had had three critically adverse days in a row and stayed in bed until the powerful conflict in her Planetary Regent was replaced by something a little less hectic.

I'd been having a pretty hectic time of my own, one way and another, only mine wasn't caused by a powerful conflict in my Planetary Regent. It was caused by seven hundred sheep that had to be manhandled one at a time through the old plunge dip. It was late by the time I'd got them all through and fished a dead ewe out of the bottom of the dip.

I started the generator up and went in for my dinner.

The breakfast dishes were still on the bench where I'd left them. Faith had been in bed all day again. I cleaned the place up a bit and I was peeling a few spuds in the sink when Faith came into the kitchen wrapped in my dressing-gown.

"Haven't you even made a cup of tea yet?" she said, feeling the teapot.

"No I bloody haven't!" I shouted at her. "And I'm not bloody going to, either!"

She looked at me for a moment or two and then burst into tears and ran to the bedroom and slammed the door and stayed in bed for another two days. That didn't seem to work either.

I tried one or two other things after that. None of them with any more success than I'd already had. I tried following the astrology stuff to the letter, at one stage. I even insisted on us eating only the recommended foods for Capricornians and Virgos. This restricted our diets to wild-carrot, wintergreen, ragwort, sage, plantain, shepherds purse, elderberry, gravel root, celery, angelica, onions, garlic, horseradish, leeks, rhubarb, wormwood, spearwort, betony and ginger. Faith got some of the stuff sent out on the R.D. van, and I brought a few things in from the station, but the whole project was doomed to failure before it started. Neither of us won or lost that one.

Another time I swiped all her astrology books when she was out of the house, and hid them. I told her I'd burnt them. But she just went to bed and stayed there until I produced them again.

That season the Blackrange Station came very close to being abandoned again. And it would have been if it hadn't been for me getting a bit of extra work around the district. I broke in horses for three big stations further down the coast and shore in a shearing gang for six weeks while Faith stayed with her folks at the motel. There were no sadistic murders of women, not locally anyway.

At the end of the year I was only eighty dollars in debt. Not bad going really, considering all the bad luck I'd had and the very unpleasant weather conditions and the lousy Stellar Configurations.

Bert's place really looked as thought it had been left out in the weather all winter and we both had a lot of cleaning up and repairing to do to keep our places farmable. The week before Christmas I seemed to get more done than I'd been able to do all year, even without the guidance of the heavenly bodies. Faith was staying on at the motel to help them prepare for the Christmas festivities.

CHAPTER FOURTEEN
FAITH IN THE FUTURE

I was so apprehensive about what the Heavenly Bodies might have up their sleeves for me this year that I took Sneak with me when I went to pick up Faith from the motel three weeks after Christmas.

As soon as I arrived I somehow got the feeling I was about as welcome as rats at a picnic.

"Oh, Kersey! What on earth did you go and bring that horrid dog with you for? You know what happens every time you bring him here."

"I lent him to a drover who'd had one of his best dogs run over," I said. "I just picked him up on my way through Pinderton."

"Well where have you been all this time? You said on the phone that you'd be here by three o'clock. What happened to you?"

I didn't like to say I'd got tied up in the pub at Pinderton over a game of darts, so I said, "Had a bit of trouble with the Hudson on the way up," instead.

"Well you'd better have your dinner. It's been in the oven for three hours."

I didn't like to say I'd had a big feed of steak and eggs after I left the pub, so I said, "Good, I'm starving."

Alby got the plate out of the oven and set it up on the table for me. Then they all went into the lounge to watch television.

I sat looking at my dinner. Three dehydrated lumps of meat and a crusted dollop of mashed potato with a thick, almost-black layer of skin on the gravy.

That afternoon I'd fed the dogs enough goat-meat to keep them going for two days, but it was worth a try. I cut off a piece of the meat and tiptoed to the back door with it and softly called Sneak. And Sneak ducked past me into the kitchen. I followed him into the room and offered him the piece of meat. He ate it without swallowing so I cut him off a bigger piece, which he also devoured. So while things were going nicely I gave him a whole piece of the stuff. The biggest bit. And Sneak took it over to the stove and put it on the floor and licked it a few times. Then he came and lay down beside my chair with a satiated groan.

I was just wiping gravy off the floor with the oven cloth when I heard them coming back from the lounge to talk to me because there was nothing worth watching on the telly.

I slapped the lump of meat on to my plate and booted Sneak out the back door and sat down again, just in time, as Alby, the old lady and Faith walked into the room.

"How's your meal, Kersey?" said Alby.

"Good as gold," I told him.

And they sat around talking to me while I ate my dinner with long teeth and murder in my heart for the treacherous Sneak.

It had been decided that Faith would stay on at the motel for a while to help out and have a holiday in civilisation at the same time. Seeing as I had Sneak with me I couldn't very well argue about it anyway, and we arranged that Faith would ring

148

up when she was ready to be collected.

I was fairly preoccupied with work on the station for a while after that, and I suddenly realised one day that it was getting on towards the end of April and I hadn't heard a word from my good keen girl.

I decided to take the matter up with Bert.

"What's the use of having a wife if she's not even here, Bert?" I said, watching his hat to see what his response would be. If he tipped it forward over his face it meant he was going to be serious. If he tipped it back he was going to try and bluff his way through, and if he put it on the side of his head he meant he was in his ribbing mood and there wouldn't be much chance of getting any sense out of him. He tipped it forward, and back, and over to one side, then the other side, then back again, and finally forward over his face and left it there and said:

"Don't see what you've got to complain about, Kersey. You're better off with her away from the place, considering what happened last year."

"Yes, I know," I said. "I'd like to know where I stand, that's all. I haven't seen or heard from her for months now."

"Do you *want* her at home?" asked Bert shrewdly.

"I don't know, Bert, and that's fair dinkum. Sometimes I think I should never have married her in the first place. It never worked out like it should have."

"Do you think you're incompatible with her then?" said Bert.

I had to think about that one for a little while.

"No, Bert," I said. "I don't think I'm incompatible with her,

149

it's her that's incompatible. She's incompatible with me, and my dogs, and my horses, and my vegetable garden, and my house — she's incompatible with the whole bloody station. She's even incompatible with the weather here. It's her that's incompatible all right."

"Well you'll just have to decide whether you want her or the station," said Bert. "Seeing as how they're so incompatible."

"I just want to know where I stand," I said.

"Well there's only one way to find out," said Bert. "You'll have to put her to the test."

"How do you mean?" I asked him.

Bert unbuckled his belt and busied himself threading it through a loop on his trousers he'd missed when he got dressed that morning. Then he carefully adjusted his hat and said:

"It's easy. Just ring her up and tell her you've got sheep dying all over the place with facial eczema and your cattle are dropping one after the other with ergot and tutu poisoning and you need a hand on the station."

"If that *was* happening Faith's the last thing I'd need," I said, "but I can see what you mean, Bert. She'll either have to come home or stay where she is."

"That's right," said Bert. "Either way you'll find out where you stand. If she refuses to come back it means she's deserted you and you've lost nothing anyway. You'll have nothing to worry about."

"What if she does decide to come back?" I said.

"In that case you *have* got something to worry about," said Bert. "Only a fat woman is any good at cooking and you've got no show of ever fattening your one."

I rang Faith up that night and told her I needed help on the station. She was quite pleasant about it and said she'd come back later on, providing I promised to get rid of Sneak.

This was a bit crook. I'd rung up to deliver an ultimatum and got slapped with one myself. I didn't want to have to choose between Faith and Sneak.

"But my dogs are the tools of my trade, in a way," I said to her. "I can't run the station without them."

"Can you run it for a little longer without me, then?" she asked.

"Sure, no trouble at all," I said.

It's November now and Faith and I have drifted apart in a kind of way. She must be enjoying her holiday at the motel, though. She's only been home to the station two or three times all year, and each time she's come with Alby and the old lady.

The first time they came the dogs were off the chain and running around. I offered to tie the dogs up and make them a cup of tea, but they were in a bit of a hurry and didn't even bother getting out of the car. We talked through the car windows about nothing in particular for a while and then they headed back for the motel.

About six weeks after that I picked up three wild cows and a wilder yearling bull on a scrubby ridge right up against the bush about three hours ride up the valley. Sneak and the good pup, Dog, took them straight down the side and they hit the riverbed and scattered out across it, bolting flat-out down the valley towards the homestead.

This was pretty good luck and by the time I got down to

where I'd left the mare tied to a log and caught up with the dogs they had the four cattle-beasts bailed up on a manuka flat only about a mile up the river from the yards. I rode in and got them moving again and within another half hour I had them more or less in a bunch near the wing that led into the stockyards. About two hundred and eighty dollars' worth, on the hoof. And I needed the money, I was already working out how I was going to spend it.

But although this was a great stroke of luck, the four cattle-beasts hadn't been worked on enough to quieten them down properly. They were still very wild and fit and spooky, while the mare and the two dogs were tired and slow from having had to cover more than three times as much ground as the cattle in order to get them where we had them. Getting them into the yards was going to be the trickiest bit.

One of the cows made a dash for the river but Sneak turned her back before she reached it, while Dog and I held the others in a bunch. I placed the two dogs out on the river side and covered the hill-side myself, and we stood there like that for a while to let the cattle quieten down a bit. Then I eased Sneak a few feet closer and the young bull moved about ten yards towards the yard gate and turned and stopped. I heeled the mare a little closer and one of the cows followed the bull. Dog pushed the other two cows over towards them.

And then the Chadwicks arrived in their Austin.

I can think of one or two things that would have been more welcome on the Blackrange Station than the Chadwicks were just then. Things like blackleg, or facial eczema, or sleepy-sickness, or distemper, or glanders, or anthrax, or foot-and-mouth, or pulpy kidney, or contagious abortion, or woody tongue, or colic, or ergot poisoning, or hydatids, or grass staggers, or blowfly strike, or black pox, or tuberculosis — or anything.

As they drove up from the road gate I slowly raised my arm to signal them to stop, but Alby didn't get the message.

He waved back at me and drove on up to the house and stopped, about forty yards away from where my four quivering cattle-beasts were milling around in a tense group at the sight of their first motorcar. Then the old lady got out of the car and they saw their first woman. Then the old lady slammed the car door and they didn't wait around to see any more. They took off for the head of the valley with their tails in the air and nothing was going to stop them.

They hit the river in a shower of spray and within a minute they were out of sight. It was no use chasing after them. They're probably still going, for all I know.

"Why are those cows running like that?" said the old lady as I rode up.

"They're in a hurry," I said.

"Kersey brings them in from the bush," explained Faith.

"I hope us arriving didn't have anything to do with them running off like that," said Alby.

"No," I said. "They were thinking of making a break for it anyway."

"Do you think they'll come back if you cut some grass and leave it out for them?" suggested the old lady.

Just then Sneak sniffed at the old lady and then wandered across to cock his leg on the wheel of their car.

"Oh look at that disgusting dog of yours, Kersey." It's no better behaved at home than when it's out. Shoo! Get away from there, you filthy thing!"

"It's his way of making you welcome," I said.

In spite of Sneak's welcome, and the fact that I didn't even get off my horse, the Chadwicks didn't stay long that time. Faith said she'd ring up if there was anything she needed, and they drove away.

The next time they came I was away up the river. When I got back there was a note on the table saying they'd stopped in to pick up one or two things of Faith's. And they sure had. Most of her clothes and gear were gone. They must have had a fair old car-load of it.

I see Faith's been drawing a few cheques on our bank in Pinderton. Costs me about one wild cattle-beast a month, but Dog is training up quite nicely on them and Bert reckons his wife costs him about the same to keep.

They want me to go through to the motel for Christmas dinner, but I don't know whether I'll bother. They'd probably put me in the unit with the scratched bench in it again. And that always reminds me of when it all started: the time when I was carried away on a tide of passion and told old lady Chadwick I reckoned her daughter was a good keen girl, when in fact I wouldn't have given the dozy bitch a job pulling ragwort for her keep.

No, I think I'll have Christmas dinner with Bert and Betty Shambles this year, like we always used to. The Chadwicks can keep their motel and their scratched bench and their good keen girl.

It was Bert and Betty who decided I needed a housekeeper. Not that I had any objections, really, but it was them who put the advertisement in the newspaper. And the phone's been ringing all morning.

Nine of them have applied for the position so far. The first one was a late Taurus. The second was Aries. The third wasn't quite sure but she thought she was Capricorn, the same as Faith, so that was the finish of that lot. The fourth was Sagittarius and the fifth and sixth were both staunch Leos. The seventh was Aquarius and obviously not very devout about it, but she had three school-age kids and required the use of a car to run around in.

The eighth was another Sagittarius and the ninth was Pisces, the fish. I still haven't had a Cancer, a Gemini, a Scorpio, a Libra or a Virgo, but it's only a matter of time.

What's wrong with the women these days? They can't always have been like this — excuse me, there's the phone ringing again.

"Kersey Hooper speaking."

"Yes, lady. That's right."

"No, the position hasn't been filled yet."

"I see."

"That sounds okay."

"No, I don't require any references. There's just one thing I'd like to know. What sign of the zodiac are you?"

"Scorpio?"

"Yes, I'm sure you are."

"Well, thanks for ringing, Mrs. Lasenby. I'll think it over and ring you back."

"Okay. Goodbye."

You see what I mean?